PRETTY LETHAL

Books by Joe Schreiber

PRETTY DEADLY

PRETTY LETHAL

JOE SCHREIBER

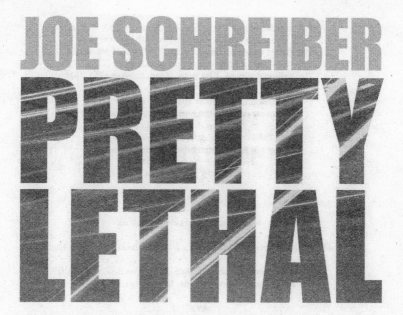

PRETTY LETHAL

First published as *Perry's Killer Playlist* in the USA in 2012
by Houghton Mifflin Harcourt Publishing Company
Published in Great Britain in 2014 by Electric Monkey,
an imprint of Egmont UK Limited
The Yellow Building, 1 Nicholas Road, London W11 4AN

Text copyright © 2012 Joe Schreiber
The moral rights of the author have been asserted

Published by special arrangement with
Houghton Mifflin Harcourt Publishing Company

ISBN 978 1 4052 5944 6

1 3 5 7 9 10 8 6 4 2

www.electricmonkeybooks.co.uk

A CIP catalogue record for this title is available from the British Library

Typeset by Avon Dataset Ltd, Bidford on Avon, Warwickshire
Printed and bound in Great Britain by CPI Group

49271/1

MIX
Paper
FSC FSC® C018306

EGMONT

Our story began over a century ago, when seventeen-year-old
Egmont Harald Petersen found a coin in the street. He was on
his way to buy a flyswatter, a small hand-operated printing
machine that he then set up in his tiny apartment.

The coin brought him such good luck that today Egmont has
offices in over 30 countries around the world. And that lucky
coin is still kept at the company's head offices in Denmark.

PROLOGUE

'American Idiot' – Green Day

'Don't kill me.'

Nine hundred feet up in the November wind, it's hard to enunciate properly, especially with the barrel of a Glock nine-millimeter jammed in your mouth. They don't tell you these things on the Travel Channel.

Gobi takes the automatic out from between my lips. Her eyes sparkle and shine. I think about what she told me back in Venice, what she said at the hotel that night. That all seems like a long time ago now.

She smiles, blood and lipstick smeared over her face. Down below, blue lights on the Champ de Mars flash off the steel framework of the Eiffel Tower, warping in the rain. Over her shoulder I can see the gendarmes on the other side of the observation platform with automatic weapons, yelling at us in the language of love. I remember just enough from two years in Mrs. Garvey's French class to decipher 'police' and 'surrender.'

'As tave myliu,' *Gobi says. With her free hand, she reaches out and brushes the wet hair out of my eyes. Her fingers are ice cold. 'Your hair is getting shaggy,* mielasis.' *Then she points the pistol back at my head.*

'Just tell me what you've done with my family.' I'm begging now, and I don't care how it sounds. 'Just tell me where they are.'

'I am so sorry, Perry.' An almost inaudible click as she switches off the safety. 'Au revoir.'

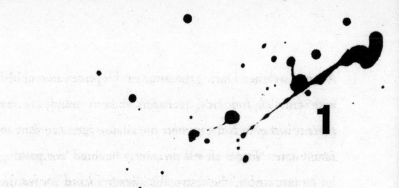

'All These Things That I've Done' – The Killers

'Miss me?' she asked.

I leaned forward to kiss the ice cream from her upper lip
– maple fudge ripple, arguably the best flavor in the known
universe. We were standing barefoot next to the picnic tables
by the Twin Star restaurant on Route 26, watching the gray
waves of October rolling up and crashing on the shore.

Me and Paula.

It was Fall, the best time of the year for this battered
stretch of shoreline that Connecticut shares with the sea. All
around us, the rest of the beach was deserted, a long,
unhurried curve of sand, eel grass and wooden fence slats
bullied and pushed over sideways by decades of rough

Atlantic weather. During the summer this place was mobbed with families and kids, teenagers, bikers, couples – my parents had even come up here on a date once, according to family lore. Now it all felt pleasantly haunted, the parking lot almost empty, the restrooms already locked up for the season, leaving the two of us and the guy behind the ice cream counter just itching to put up his handwritten SEE YOU NEXT SUMMER! sign in the window.

High above us, seagulls squeaked and wheeled in the gunmetal sky, sounding lost and far away.

Paula hugged herself and shivered. 'It's chilly.'

'Here.' I took off my Columbia sweatshirt and wrapped it around her shoulders. 'Better?'

'Always the gentleman.' She smiled and looked down at the beach, her cell phone still clutched in her hand from the call that she'd just finished. 'So, do you want to hear the big news?'

'I thought you'd never tell me.'

'I thought you'd never ask.'

'Officially asking.'

'I just got off the phone with Armitage . . . and he wants to book Inchworm . . .' she paused, making me wait an

4

extra split-second . . . 'for the whole tour.'

'Europe?'

'Twelve cities in eighteen days.'

'No way!' I laughed, and she grabbed me, and I hugged her, lifting her up off her feet and spinning her around. 'Paula, that's unbelievable.'

'I know!' Her smile had blossomed into a full-out grin, and I looked at all eleven of the sun freckles across the bridge of her nose. I'd counted them when we were waiting in line for one of the rides at Six Flags last month.

'How did that happen?'

'I told you the new songs were great, Perry. Armitage heard your demo and flipped.' Now she was clutching my hands, bouncing up and down on her tiptoes with excitement. Her toenails were painted a very dark shade of plum, almost black, and they looked great against the sand, ten little black keys, like the kind you use to play ragtime. 'He's booking you guys on a twelve-city tour, starting in London on the twenty-ninth, then Venice, Paris, Madrid . . .' Paula got out her phone, clicking up the screen. 'I've got all the dates here.'

'This is amazing,' I said. 'I can't wait to see Europe with you.'

She sighed softly, and her shoulders sagged a little. 'I wish.'

'Wait – you're not coming?'

'Armitage needs me here in New York. And I've got to be back in the studio at the beginning of December. Moby's recording a new album in L.A., and . . .' She saw my expression. 'Hey, maybe I can sneak out to Paris for a weekend.'

'I'd like that.'

'Perry, this is a huge step for you guys. If this works out . . .'

I smiled. 'I couldn't have done it without you.'

'Oh, shut up.'

'I'm serious,' I said. 'You made this happen.'

'Well, that's sweet of you to say.' Her blue eyes sparkled, appearing and disappearing as her hair blew in front of her face. She'd spent most of the summer in L.A. and somehow held on to her tan into the Fall, so that her blond hair looked even blonder by comparison. 'But we all know who really deserves the credit.'

'Stop it.'

'You wrote all of those new songs, Perry.'

'Norrie and I wrote them together.'

'Then you and Norrie are the next Lennon and McCartney,' she said. 'And now the entire European Union is going to find that out for themselves.'

'This is amazing.'

'I know.' She frowned a little, seeing the hint of apprehension in my eyes. 'What?'

'Nothing – it's just great news.'

'Stormaire . . .'

I smiled. 'I just wish you could go with me, that's all.'

'You're adorable.' She kissed me again, and the kiss lingered this time, her mouth warm and soft against mine, her hair tickling my ears.

'I know.'

She stood there looking at me. We'd been dating for less than three months, but I'd told her everything, and she could read me like a book.

'Europe's a big continent, Perry.'

'I know.'

'You don't even know if she's there.'

'Right.'

'It's not like you're going to run into her.'

'I never said – '

'You didn't have to.'

'I wasn't even thinking it.'

'There's a reason why I'm not sending you guys to Lithuania,' Paula said, and squeezed my hand. 'Come on. I'm cold. Let's walk.'

2

'Ever Fallen in Love' – Buzzcocks

Paula and I had met back in the beginning of August, at a party in Park Slope, not long after I'd seen Gobi for the last time on the steps at Columbia. It turned out that I didn't really know a lot of people at the party, one of those friend-of-a-friend-who-wasn't-really-a-friend type of things. Someone kept playing old Elton John tracks on the iPod docking station, and I was in the process of saying my goodbyes when a voice I'd never heard before said, 'Hey.'

That was how she'd started out, as a voice over my shoulder, sounding raspy and unfamiliar and amused. 'You're that guy,' the voice said.

I turned around to look at her, my brain immediately

struggling to crunch the numbers. Laid out on the chalkboard, it would've gone something like this:

(blond hair) + (blue eyes) x (killer body) = don't even try

Yet here was this woman, a little older than I was and a whole lot hotter, not only looking at me but actually seeming interested.

'I'm sorry?'

'I saw your picture in the *Post*,' she said. 'You're Perry Stormaire, right?'

'Yeah.'

'You're the guy whose house got blown up.'

'Uh-huh.'

'That was insane.'

'Yes,' I said, because I never know what to say in these situations. She was referring to what happened on the night of my senior prom, three months before, when the Lithuanian foreign exchange that had been living in our house – a girl named Gobija Zaksauskas – turned out to be an assassin with a hit list of names. With Gobi's gun to my head, we'd spent the night careening around New York City in my father's Jaguar while she killed her targets one by one, ending with my house getting blown up. Describing the night as 'insane' could arguably be considered an insult to the mentally ill.

'Your family was all right?'

'Yes.'

'And they never found that woman's body?'

'Destroyed in the fire,' I said. 'That's what they think, anyway.'

'Wow.' We stood there for a moment, and she seemed to realize that she hadn't introduced herself. 'I'm Paula Daniels.'

She held out her hand, and I shook it in that smiling, somewhat awkward way that people shake hands when they're flirting, and it occurred to me that that's what we were doing. When a couple of people stepped past us on their way through the door, Paula edged a little closer, her bare shoulder brushing against my arm, and the party noise seemed to fade way down in the mix so it was as if just the two of us were standing there talking to each other. Something happened right then. It was that weightless moment when you stop worrying about riding the bike and just starting riding it.

'Can I ask you a personal question?' she said.

'Sure.'

'Was it all true?'

'Are you kidding?' I said. 'I couldn't have made that stuff up.'

'I had a feeling.' A tiny smile touched the corner of her lips and echoed in her eyes with a shimmer that I could almost hear, like the soft chime of an incoming text message. 'I pride myself on my ability to separate truth and bullshit.'

'That's a rare talent,' I said.

'Not as marketable as it used to be.'

'Maybe you should be a detective.'

She laughed an easy, natural laugh. 'I bet you get asked that a lot.'

'What?'

'You know – fact or fiction.'

'Actually, no,' I said. 'It's weird, but most people don't really seem to care.'

And it was true. They had read about what happened with me and Gobi on prom night in New York in the newspapers and seen it on TV, posted about it on their blogs, forwarded it and 'liked' it on Facebook and tweeted

12

about it to their friends. As far as the American public was concerned, what happened to us that night was the truth, yet another improbable chunk of 'reality' gone viral in a post-MTV world, and everybody had just kind of accepted it and moved on.

'So you're not a detective,' I said.

'No.'

'What do you do besides read the *Post* and go to parties in Brooklyn?'

She smiled, cocked an eyebrow. 'There's more to life?'

'Depends who you ask, I guess.'

'Fair enough. The truth is, I work in the music industry.'

I felt my heart do a little stumble-step in my chest, because this conversation really did seem to be entering the department of Too Good to Be True. 'Really.'

'Yes.'

'You know,' I said, 'that's funny, because I sort of play in a band.'

'Inchworm.' Paula nodded. 'I remember from the story.'

'Yeah.' I was starting to think I could really fall in love with this girl. 'Well, ah, anyway . . . we all decided to take a year off before college, just to see if we can make something happen. If not . . .' I shrugged.

'If you don't try, you'll always wonder.'

I nodded. 'Exactly.'

'You should slip me your demo.'

'Seriously?'

'Absolutely. I work for this European promoter, George Armitage – '

'Wait a second,' I said. '*The* George Armitage?'

'That's him.'

'Are you kidding? Armitage is, like, the hottest promoter in the world right now. Ever since the Enigma festival in the U.K. last summer, plus he owns his own airline . . . You actually work for that guy?'

Paula smiled. 'Well, I'm sort of the liaison between him and the labels. Technically I'm on Armitage's payroll, but I spend about half my time in L.A., working with new bands in the studio. It's kind of a position that I created for myself.'

'That sounds amazing.'

'I grew up in Laurel Canyon.' Paula reached up, tucked a strand of hair behind her ear. 'My father was an A&R guy back in the day, worked with all the legends – Fleetwood

Mac, Steely Dan, the Eagles. Madonna and Sean Penn practically got a divorce in our pool. It's in my blood.'

And that was how it started. People talk about fate and luck and blind chance, and even now I'm not sure where I stand on those issues, but I will say this: In the weeks and months that Paula and I got more serious, I found her to be exactly as confident, ambitious, imaginative, and funny as she was that first night, and as I got to know her better, I sort of ran out of adjectives. She was that mixed mouthful of flavors, the kind of person that would walk through a farmer's market and in the middle of a conversation about Soviet cinema in the 1940s, pick up two bananas and pretend they were her eyebrows.

And she was unfathomably beautiful, totally out of my league. The kind of girl you write songs about. She was twenty-two years old, and I was eighteen.

Then again, historically, I tend to prefer older women.

3

'Is There Something I Should Know?' – Duran Duran

But hows the sex????

I looked at my iPhone, knowing the message was from Norrie before I even got a look at the screen. He was the only one that texted me on a regular basis, even though we saw each other practically every day at practice. Everybody else – including Sasha, our lead singer, and Caleb, our guitarist – just called.

It's awesome, I typed.

```
how awesme?
```

```
Tantric.
```

A long pause, and then:

```
yr still not getting any, r u?
```

'Who are you texting?' Paula asked from the driver's seat.

I switched off the phone and stuffed it in my pocket. 'Norrie.'

'Did you tell him yet?'

'I told him there's a band meeting at my house in an hour. I want it to be a surprise. Unless Linus already talked to them.' Linus Feldman was our manager, a five-foot-two, hundred-and-eight-pound Jewish tsunami who'd blown in sometime last summer from the wilds of Staten Island. He was old-school management, a scarred veteran of a dozen legendary management teams from back in the go-go eighties, when rock-and-roll was minting millionaires on what seemed like a weekly basis. From the moment he'd come out of semi-retirement to represent Inchworm, he'd been waiting for someone to try to take advantage of us so he could rip their head off. So far, to his great disappointment, we'd been treated with an unprecedented level of fairness and respect.

'I'm not sure how crazy Linus is about the idea.'

'A European tour? How could he not be thrilled?'

'He's got his own ideas about the band,' Paula said. 'We'll see how it goes.'

She signaled left and turned from the beach road onto the two-lane highway and I watched the ocean receding in my side-view mirror, each of us lost in our own thoughts.

I checked my phone to see if I might have missed any more texts, but the last one was from Norrie, accusing me of not yet having sex with Paula. Unfortunately, he was right. Paula and I had spent hours on the couch, kissing until our lips were numb and tingling, and we'd done plenty of other stuff, basically everything you can do – but the Deed itself remained undone.

It definitely wasn't Paula's fault. She'd made it pretty clear that she was ready whenever I was, which I guess made me one of the worst deal-closers of all time. Throughout junior high and high school, all I'd thought about was the day I'd finally get rid of the virginity problem. Now here was Paula with her knockout face and smoking body – an experienced woman, no less – patiently waiting to teach me so that I wouldn't knee-and-elbow my way through the chicken dance of sexual initiation the way my parents' generation had, decoding the lyrics of bad eighties hair-metal power ballads as our Kama Sutra. Exactly what did you say to a girl after she shook you all night long? And was pouring some sugar on someone as sticky as it sounded?

We were an enlightened generation. Chow had lost his cherry to his girlfriend back in his sophomore year of high school, Sasha and Caleb had never had any problems scoring ('Dude,' Sasha once said, with absolute sincerity, 'why do you think we even play in a band?'), and even Norrie sounded like he was at it pretty routinely with his current girlfriend. Here I was, paralyzed at the starting line, waiting. For what? True love? A sign from God? A long weekend in Paris?

Therapy was what I needed, and a lot of it. Meanwhile, I wondered if there was a Virgins Anonymous program in some church basement somewhere, or at least a cult in southern Connecticut in need of one to sacrifice.

Throughout it all, Paula remained super cool about the whole thing. She always said she'd wait until I was ready. But how long before her anticipation turned to exasperation?

Meanwhile, I tried not to think about it.

It was a great plan, and sometimes it almost worked.

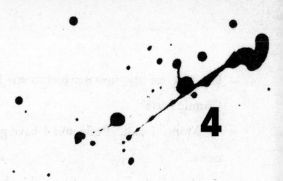

4

'The Loved Ones' – Elvis Costello and the Attractions

When we got back to the house, Mom was in the kitchen with her laptop and a glass of wine. We'd just moved in at the end of the summer – the workmen were still finishing the addition over the garage, and there were color tiles spread out on every surface, two thousand shades of white. It looked like a Michael Bolton concert on our kitchen table.

'Hi, Perry. Oh, hello, Paula. How was the beach?'

'It was great.'

'I've always loved that stretch of shoreline, especially in the Fall.' She cast her gaze across at the sea of nearly identical rectangles fanned out across the table. 'Which color do you like best for the upstairs bathroom, honey? Isabelline or Cosmic Latte?'

'Mom,' I said, 'Paula and I have got some really great news.'

Mom looked up, her face suddenly slack with surprise. 'You're not getting married, are you?'

'What? *No.*'

'Thank God.' Mom reached for her wine glass. 'I mean, not that you're not a wonderful, terrific person, Paula, but –'

'It's all right, Mrs. Stormaire,' Paula said, and flicked her eyes in my direction. She still hadn't gotten to the point where she could comfortably call my mom 'Julie' yet. 'For a second there, the way Perry said that, I think I almost had a heart attack too.'

'So I assume that means you're also not . . .' Mom gestured with her hands in front of her stomach.

'What?' I said. 'Full?'

'You know what I mean.'

'Seriously, Mom?'

'Honey, I'm sorry, but these are the thoughts that run through a mother's mind.' And before I could ask her why they had to be the thoughts that ran out of her mouth, she was back on the laptop, clicking away, talking and typing at the same time. 'You know, I was thinking, since this is going to be our first Thanksgiving in the new house, and Paula, I know that your family is out in California . . . would you like to come and have Thanksgiving with us?'

I took a deep breath. 'I might not be around for Thanksgiving.'

The typing noise stopped. From here I could see that she'd been updating her Facebook page, and in the silence I could feel her status changing. 'Oh?'

'I was trying to tell you – '

'Tell us what?' That was Dad, coming down the stairs and around the corner with his iPhone in his hand and the *Times* under his arm. Immediately reading a disturbance in the emotional weather of the room, he turned to my mother. 'What's wrong?'

'I don't know.' Mom was frowning, and two red spots had appeared on her cheeks. 'Your son hasn't told me yet.'

'Perry?' My father put on his stern attorney voice. 'What's going on?'

'Look,' I started, and that was probably a good start, but

at that moment, the rusty Econoline van came squealing up into our driveway and I saw Norrie and Caleb jump out and start lugging their guitar cases and drums up toward our garage with the unquestioning sense of purpose that comes from not being able to go anywhere without hauling five hundred pounds of equipment along. We'd been using my house for practice for the past couple weeks, and they must have assumed that my announcement of tonight's meeting was business as usual.

'I should go talk to those guys.'

'Maybe you should wait,' Paula said.

'Why?'

She pointed out the window, not that it was necessary. There was no mistaking the tubercular gargle of the vehicle as it charged down the street and pulled in behind the van and Paula's car. Linus Feldman drove a burgundy 1996 Olds 88, its chassis rusted and flaking down the primer, its remaining paint the color of an old bruise. Linus's car doubled as his office, meaning the passenger seat was usually overflowing with unanswered correspondence, disputed contracts and flyers for our shows, past and future. Stepping out, he emerged in a swirl of paperwork and Starbucks cups.

'Stormaire?' he bellowed, arriving at the front door without bothering to knock. 'Is Paula in there? Send that duplicitous wench out here now.'

Paula sighed.

'Linus?' Dad blinked. 'What's he doing here?'

Having trumpeted his arrival in no uncertain terms, Linus stood on our porch, arms crossed, with the air of a man who could wait forever. He was floating in a corduroy suit jacket with suede elbow patches and khaki pants, and his fluffy white popcorn hair seemed to swell, doubling and tripling with the sheer ferocity of his indignation.

I opened the door. 'Hi, Linus.'

'Did you sign a contract?'

'No, I – '

'But you've seen it.'

'A contract for what?' Dad asked, alternating his attention between me and Linus. He knew that Linus was a lawyer like himself, a brotherhood with an overlap that might ideally permit them to use some kind of professional shorthand, although on the few occasions when they'd met, it seemed to work the opposite way, signals crossing, interfering with each other's frequencies. 'Perry, what's going on?'

'Take it easy, Linus,' Paula said. 'Let's all just breathe.'

'Don't patronize me, Yoko.' Linus held up a sheet of paper, thrusting it in our faces as if it were a warrant for someone's arrest. 'An e-mail from George Armitage's assistant? *This* is how I find out that you're taking Inchworm on a European tour?'

'That was an oversight,' Paula said. 'George was supposed to let me tell you myself.'

'This is completely unacceptable.'

'Wait – '

'Europe?' Mom said. 'Perry? When were you planning on telling us about this?'

Dad reached for the e-mail in Linus's hand. 'May I see this, please?'

'These terms are absurd,' Linus said, snatching the e-mail away before any of us could see it. 'You can tell George Armitage that he can take his tour and shove it up his – '

'Perry's never been out of the country before,' Mom said.

'That's not true,' I said. 'I went to Toronto for the Shakespeare festival my junior year. And we all went to

Paradise Island for Christmas that year. My passport's up to date.'

'Okay.' Paula took in a deep breath. 'With all due respect, I think we're focusing on the wrong things here.'

'For once we're in perfect agreement.' Linus put his arm around my shoulder and led me aside, lowering his voice. 'Perry, you know I respect you. You know I want what's right for the band. I'll go to the mat for you every single time.' He held his head as if it were in danger of flying apart. 'But these terms – '

'What about if we all went with you?' Mom said. 'We'd stay out of your way, let you play your shows . . .'

'Wait.' That was Annie, from all the way upstairs in her bedroom, where she'd apparently been monitoring the entire conversation through the ductwork. 'We're going to *Europe?*'

At that moment the entire east wing of the house exploded with the heavy, chugging drum and guitar notes that meant Caleb and Norrie had plugged in and were warming up at top volume, waiting for me to come out and join them. Sasha, our lead singer, wasn't here yet – he was always the last to arrive, and, ever since he'd bought a vintage

Indian motorcycle that broke down every other week, it wasn't uncommon for him to show up in his mom's Volvo, or even on a bicycle.

'Family summit.' Annie moved past me in a cloud of conflicting perfumes and hair treatment smells. 'Oh, hi, Linus.' She looked at my dad. 'Are we going to Europe?'

'No,' Dad said.

'How come Perry gets to go?'

'Don't worry, sweetheart,' Linus said, glaring over her head at Paula. 'Uncle Linus isn't going to let the evil lady take anybody to Europe for this kind of chump change.'

'Perry's going on tour,' Mom said, 'with his band. Isn't that exciting?'

Annie rolled her eyes. 'I'm all a-flutter.' Irony was her new ketchup, and she was putting it on everything.

'I think I'd better take a look at that contract,' Dad said, reaching for his reading glasses, which weren't in his breast pocket.

'Don't bother,' Linus said, and his hands had gone from his head to his stomach. His initial wave of outrage had passed, leaving him with what looked like chronic dyspepsia. 'Just let me kick you in the balls and you'll get the idea.'

'Linus,' Paula said, 'I know this is your preferred method of negotiation, but – '

'Negotiation?' Linus wailed, flung back by the very apogee of disbelief. 'What is there to negotiate? How am I supposed to negotiate with *nothing?'*

'In case you didn't notice,' Paula said, putting her arm around me, 'I'm on Perry's side here. I'm kind of crazy about the guy.'

'Oh, that's rich. You're good.' He waved his hands to anyone who might listen. '*She's* good. This is worse than the Jacksons' Victory Tour back in eighty-four, when we had to leave Tito in Vancouver.'

'Linus, that's enough,' I said. 'Let's just listen to what she has to say, okay?'

'This is how it starts,' Linus moaned. 'This is how it always starts . . .'

Out in the garage, the guitar and drums had stopped, and I heard Caleb and Norrie come blundering inside, Cokes in hand, to find out what was taking me so long. They saw Linus standing there with Paula and my folks and stopped in their tracks.

'Hey, dude,' Norrie said. 'What's up?'

'I think you'll find that the terms are boilerplate for any new band with no track record internationally,' Paula said. 'Armitage is working out the merchandising deals with promoters for shirts and promotional items, and the exposure for Inchworm – '

Caleb blinked. 'What's she talking about, Perry?'

There was a clattering noise, and I looked out the window and saw that Sasha had arrived. He was wearing leather pants and a feather-plumed boa and pedaling the old twelve-speed Schwinn, which meant that his motorcycle had broken down yet again and was drooling oil somewhere in the back of his mom's garage – but for once, none of these setbacks seemed to be bothering him in the least. Instead, he leapt off the bike while it was still rolling, letting it rattle to a halt into our garbage cans, and came sprinting up my front steps, bursting into the house, taking in the sight of me and Caleb and Norrie with a huge grin on his face.

'Did you guys hear?' He pumped his fists. 'Did Linus tell you? We're going to Europe, bitches!'

'Wait,' Caleb said. 'Whaaaat?'

Norrie's mouth dropped open. 'Seriously?'

'Hell, yeah! Inchworm's first world tour! Linus says once

he negotiates the contract it's gonna put us over the top, and – ' He turned around. 'Oh, hey, Linus.'

Linus dropped his face in his hands. Through his fingers I could hear him murmuring to himself, praying for strength to persevere in the face of insurmountable obstacles – first among them the band that he'd agreed to represent.

'So,' Paula said, 'can I call Armitage and tell him we have a deal?'

5

'You Are a Tourist' – Death Cab for Cutie

'Man,' Norrie said, 'anybody else feel like wuh-we've been doing this for about tuh-ten years already?'

It was eight-thirty at night, Italian time, and the Inchworm European tour had just rolled into Venice's Santa Lucia station – meaning that we were lugging our own gear down onto the platform, having spent the better part of the last two days on the train playing Nintendo DS and trying not to drive each other crazy.

Time had become a blur. With Linus leading the way, we'd left London yesterday at midday, taken the Chunnel into Paris, and left after lunch today to go to Venice.

Things had started out a little shaky. At our first gig in

London, Caleb couldn't find his Stratocaster, Norrie was still sick from the airline food, and half our amps weren't wired to run off European power outlets. Backstage, Linus was pacing a hole in the dressing room floor, chain-smoking some obscure brand of foul-smelling British cigarettes while reassuring everybody that it was going to be okay. Outside, the crowd was getting antsy while the roadies fiddled with the amplifiers until finally, at a quarter past nine, Sasha stood up and said screw it, he didn't know about the rest of us, but he for one hadn't flown halfway around the world to sit in some dressing room like a bunch of American losers.

Then we went out there and rocked.

In the end it had taken approximately thirty seconds to realize what we should've known from the start: When the four of us got together, it didn't matter if we were playing in New York, in London, or on the moon – when it came right down to it, at this particular moment in our lives, when our backs were to the wall, we could set that shit on fire.

Even with half the amps off, Caleb's loaner guitar squealed and soloed like the devil's own chainsaw, Sasha was pulling out moves that none of us had ever seen before, spoonfeeding the crowd until they were shrieking for more, and Norrie sounded like he was setting off cherry bombs in the drum kit. We roared through every song on the set list, including a few new ones that we'd only practiced a couple times, until even the bouncers came up front and started dancing. Midway through the show, I glanced back at Norrie and saw him grinning back at me, a perfect reflection of that slightly dazed feeling of wonder. *This is real,* we were both thinking, at the exact same time. *Holy shit, this is actually happening to us right now.*

Up front, Sasha gave his patented Navajo war whoop and a flying helicopter kick that just cleared the microphone stand. 'Hello, U.K.!' he yelled. 'We are Inchworm and we are here to rock you – 'kay?'

The place went absolutely bonkers. Finally, after playing almost three straight hours and closing with a rousing cover of Sham 69's 'If the Kids Are United' that had the whole place up on its feet and singing along, we stumbled offstage, exhausted and soaked with sweat, grinning like fools, and collapsed into a black cab back to the hotel with a couple of girls from the front row. I called Paula in New York and told her how it had gone, while Sasha leaned out the window and howled, 'Who wants to do that again?'

We all did.

• . •·.•

Now, forty-four hours later, we were here in Venice. Two steps off the train, Norrie dropped his duffle bag on the platform next to Caleb's and flung himself down on it as if it were a huge body pillow, pulling down his baseball cap and closing his eyes. Linus had fought his way into the station to buy tickets for the water taxi, and Sasha had tagged along, already on the prowl for Italian girls. Of the four of us, he was the only one with a seemingly limitless supply of energy, propelled forward by the libido of an adolescent rhino.

I was digging through my bag for the last Red Bull when my phone started ringing. I looked at the screen and saw an international number I didn't recognize.

'Hello?'

'Perry?'

'Yes.'

'George Armitage here. How are you, mate?'

I stood up a little straighter, suddenly feeling wide awake. 'Oh. I'm – I'm fine.' Even after all the time I'd been with Paula and talked about Armitage, what he was like and so on, I'd never actually spoken to the man.

'How's the tour going so far?'

'It's going great. We were in London . . . It's been incredible – '

'Splendid. Love the new songs, honestly. The reviews of the London show have been over the moon. You blokes are going to be huge – you do realize that, don't you?'

'Thanks,' I said. In front of me, Caleb and Norrie were now both sprawled out on their bags. They looked like they'd gone into matching comas. Norrie was drooling.

'You're in Venice now, aren't you?' Armitage asked.

'That's right. We just got in.'

'Brilliant, brilliant. Wish I could be there to show you the city.'

'Yeah, that would be cool.' For a split second I toyed with the idea of asking him where he was, but I managed to stop the question from tumbling off my lips. According to Paula, George Armitage was an intensely private man. If you Googled him – and we all had – you'd find out that he was

British by birth but had renounced his British citizenship and spent most of his time traveling, a media multi-hyphenate. Nobody was quite sure where all his money had come from. In recent years he'd expanded his operation globally and become, for all intents and purposes, his own free-floating sovereign nation. He ran his own production company, a publishing group, and an airline. By all accounts he had more cash than he knew what to do with.

'While you're traveling, if there's anything you need, I hope you won't hesitate to ask.'

'Thank you,' I said, unable to shake the feeling that there must have been some other reason he'd decided to call. I didn't have to wait long to find out what it was.

'Listen, mate. I didn't want to mention anything too early, but at this rate, there might be a record deal for you at the end of all of this.'

I felt my heart stop. 'Seriously?'

'Absolutely,' Armitage said. 'Ask Paula. The last band whose tour I set up sold six million units in the first two months. Legends are forged by fire. We'll speak soon. Cheers.'

I said goodbye, turned, and kicked Norrie's duffle bag

until he pushed himself up on his elbows, blinking, and gave me the finger. 'Whuh-what the hell's wrong with you, Stormaire?'

'George Armitage just called me. He wants to get us a record deal.'

'Armitage?' Norrie stared at me. All at once he didn't look remotely tired. Caleb sat up next to him. 'What? *Now?*'

'Come on,' I said. 'Let's go find Linus.'

They were both on their feet already and grabbed their bags, and I hoisted my guitar case, following them down the platform, my head whirling with what Armitage had said and with the abrupt influx of noise and commotion inside the train station.

6

'Another Girl, Another Planet' – The Replacements

The whole thing happened so fast that I almost didn't realize what was happening until it was over. One moment I was following Caleb and Norrie through the automatic sliding doors into the main terminal, and the next, I was alone in the crowd.

I turned around and looked back in the direction I'd come, thinking maybe I'd somehow gotten ahead of them, but they weren't back there. Off to my left was a big café, and somewhere to my right was a row of ticket windows. I didn't see Linus or any of the others up there. People buzzed by in every direction, wheeling luggage, toting backpacks. None of them was familiar.

Ten minutes in Venice and I was already lost.

        •   • • •

I walked out of the station and down the gray steps leading to the Grand Canal, then stopped in my tracks.

Not until that moment did it really hit me that I was in a city that had rivers instead of streets and boats instead of cars. There were intersections, alleyways, and bridges with gondolas tied up to them. Up above the half-submerged doorways and steps I saw ancient stone hotels and ruined palaces sinking into the lagoon. Fog hung over the surface, seagulls dipping and flicking up the waterway, their bellies glinting white and then disappearing in the dark.

I bought a twenty-four-hour pass for the vaporetto, got on the next boat, and called Norrie.

'Dude,' he said, 'whuh-what happened to you? We thought we luh-lost you for good.'

'I'm fine. I just lost you guys at the train station.'

'Whuh-Where are you now?'

'The Grand Canal.' I was standing on the deck of a vaporetto with my bag and my guitar case, heading down the canal. Overhead, high gothic arches and crumbling statuary moved slowly past on either side, lit from within like a Pirates of the Caribbean ride. Define *lame:* I was in Venice, and all I could think of was Disney World. 'I'll meet you at the hotel.'

'Yuh-You buh-better. Linus is fuh-freaking out.'

'Tell him to calm down. I'll be there in an hour or so.'

'It's the Puh-Pensione Guerrato,' he said, 'by the Ruh-Rialto Bridge.'

'Got it.'

'Whuh-What are you duh-*doing?*'

'Seeing the sights.'

'It's luh-like ten o'clock at nuh-night!'

'Relax, okay? I'll catch up to you later.'

Norrie fell quiet for just a second, and when he spoke again, there was no trace of a stutter in his voice.

'You're going to look for her, aren't you?'

I drew in a breath. I don't know whether it was the unwavering certainty in his voice or just that we'd been friends for so long, but I knew instantly that I couldn't lie to him.

'Maybe.'

He made an exasperated lip-fart. 'Whuh-What about Puh-Paula?'

'What about her?' my answer came back, probably too quickly. 'It's not like I'm cheating on her. I probably won't even find Gobi anyway, but if I do, we'll have a cup of coffee, catch up for a few minutes, and that's it.'

'Buh-Bullshit.'

'Hey, believe what you want.'

'Thuh-This is a ruh-really buh-bad idea.'

I took in a breath and let it out. 'Yeah. I know.'

'I nuh-*know* you know,' Norrie said miserably. 'Juh-Just like I know yuh-you're going to duh-do it anyway.' He was silent again for a moment. 'Shit. At least tuh-tell her wuh-we said hello.' Then, with more conviction: 'And duh-don't stuh-stay out all nuh-night! Wuh-We've got a gig tomorrow!'

'Okay,' I said, and hung up.

$$\bullet \quad \bullet \quad \bullet$$

Up ahead I saw what looked like the open lagoon, the boat nudging its way up to the San Marco stop. On the shore, two guys in long dark coats and immaculate pointy-toed leather shoes were smoking and sipping espressos out of paper cups by the dock.

'Excuse me.' My voice came out froggy and hoarse, like I was getting a cold. 'I'm looking for Harry's Bar.'

'Like Hemingway, *si*?'

'Yeah,' I said. 'I mean, I guess.'

The first man smiled and said something, and they both laughed.

'I'm sorry, I don't speak Italian.'

'He said that even an idiot American could find that place from here,' the other man said, and as they turned and started walking away, I saw the sign behind them in the window, in art deco letters: HARRY'S BAR.

Now that it was right in front of me, I wasn't sure that I was ready to go in. I walked around the corner to the side of the building that faced the canal. Standing on my tiptoes, I could just see inside, where a group of fashionably dressed patrons were sitting at the bar.

This was it.

A voice in my head whispered, *Do you really want to do this?*

But I was already walking inside.

7

'Waiting for Somebody' – Paul Westerberg

Harry's was a long yellow room, warm and dry, with dark wooden tables glowing beneath wall sconces and an old metal fan in the corner. The bar itself was only long enough for the half-dozen patrons that I'd seen through the window, gathered together talking and laughing as if they had known one another all their lives. The bartender was wearing a pressed white tuxedo jacket. When I walked in, he didn't say anything, just gazed at my wet jeans and windbreaker, and the guitar case at my feet.

'Can I get a Mountain Dew or something?'

'Mountain . . . Do?'

'Or a Coke?'

A sigh. '*Si*, Coke.'

I sat down at the end of the bar next to a glass cabinet of souvenirs for sale and sipped my ten-euro Coke, staring at the door. I didn't know what I was doing here.

Gobi and I had talked about Harry's Bar back in New York, as some fantasy rendezvous point in a future that neither one of us had ever expected would be real. Now that I was actually here, though, things seemed different, and I couldn't stop thinking about how it would be if she really did show up. What if the night that we'd spent together had been a once-in-a-lifetime phenomenon, a potent but irreproducible mixture of hormones and gunpowder, never to be repeated? What would we say to each other – would there even be anything to say?

'*Signori?*'

I jumped and looked up from my drink, and realized the bartender was staring at me.

'We are closing for the night.'

I looked at the clock over the bar. It was five to eleven. That seemed early, but I saw that the other patrons had left or were putting on their coats and scarves, paying their tabs, saying goodbye, heading out into the cold Venetian night.

'Can I just hang out here a few more minutes?' I asked.

He sighed. *'Si.'*

I sat while the waiters wiped down the tables, put away glasses, and started turning off the lights around me, *click, click, click*. By now the bar had emptied out entirely. The bartender reappeared in front of me wearing his own coat, his face very serious now.

'Signori, I am sorry, but we must close.'

'Okay.' I got out my wallet, dug out the emergency Visa card, and paid the tab. 'Thank you.'

'Prego.' The waiter let me out and locked the door behind me.

I stepped out. The rain was falling harder now, the wind gusting it straight into my face, and there was no one on the street in front of the canal. I thought about what I'd read about Venice sinking. Everywhere I looked, the lagoon was lapping up the steps and filling the doorways. Up ahead, I saw two men – the same ones in suits, smoking, that I'd talked to before – emerge out in front of me as if they'd been there waiting for me the whole time.

'So you found it,' one of them said.

'What?'

'Your little tourist trap.'

I turned and started walking in the other direction, and another man with a shaved head appeared in front of me, blocking my way, his gaze shifting up to the two behind my back. The bald one was young, wearing jeans and a shiny, puffy black coat that seemed like it was stitched together out of designer garbage bags. A second later I felt something hard and cold jab up against the back of my neck. Over my shoulder I could smell garlic and cigarettes mixed with overpowering cologne. One hand grabbed my shoulder, slamming me face-first into the alley wall hard enough that I heard my incisors scrape off the concrete before I hit the ground. Pain burst through the left side of my face and I tasted blood, salty and fresh, as fingers rifled my back pocket, yanking out my wallet.

'Just take whatever you want,' I said, my tongue flicking off my newly chipped tooth. 'Just – '

'Where is she?'

'What?' I said. *'Who?'*

Then one of the men screamed.

All at once I heard feet scuffling above me and a series of quick, brutal thumps, like a glove stuffed with pennies smacking into flesh. Someone grunted, staggered, fell, and footsteps went slapping fast up the alley, through the puddles, and then there was no sound except for the rain.

'I see you have still not learned to fight.'

I looked up.

Gobi was standing in the alley in front of me, hands on her hips, with two of the men sprawled at her feet. For a second I didn't know if what I was seeing was real or just a delayed result of head trauma.

She was wearing a short leather jacket with lots of buckles, and some kind of stretchy black micro-skirt, torn black stockings, and big chunky shitkicker boots. Her hair was dyed and chopped above the shoulders.

'How did you find me?' I asked.

'Perry.' She shook her head. 'You do not look so good.'

'Yeah, well, I could've used you . . .' – I stopped and coughed hard, looked at my hand, and saw a little spatter of scarlet across my knuckles – 'like, about twenty seconds earlier?'

'So use me now.' She extended one hand and I took it, lifting myself up. I was still getting my balance when she leaned forward, catching me in her arms, and I saw the little white scar across her neck, and all the rest of it came back from there.

8

'Never Let Me Down Again' – Depeche Mode

We crossed a dark bridge to the Centurion Palace Hotel. It was a sleek slice of L.A.-style architecture built inside what looked like a five-hundred-year-old palace on the opposite side of the canal, and to get inside we had to cross a wide courtyard of perfectly oval stones that crunched under our feet as we walked over them. She led me into a high-domed lobby with a chandelier made of curved glass tubes and long sofas arranged across the wide marble floor. From the concierge desk I saw a pair of high-cheekboned faces, incurious and androgynous, peering back at us from a liquid cloud of blue light.

'Lift is this way,' she said. 'Follow me.'

I stepped into the brushed chrome elevator, feeling it rise smoothly upward, transporting us to some upper floor. There, Gobi kept me walking forward down the silent corridor. She swiped her keycard and we entered her suite, a series of rooms, one flowing into the next, opening out toward a balcony overlooking the canal. I saw a bottle of champagne on ice in front of the flat-screen TV, the counter scattered with her BlackBerry, jewelry, a jumbled pile of euros and foreign coins, her passport and lipstick.

'Take off your clothes.'

'What?'

'You are freezing with the cold.'

'Look, I should probably tell you something.' I managed to get the windbreaker off, turning one of the sleeves inside out as I pulled my arm free, then reached down to unbutton my pants. 'Do you mind looking the other way?'

She cocked one eyebrow, then turned to face the wall as I peeled off my jeans, then my socks, and finally my T-shirt. 'I'm involved with somebody. She's back in the States.'

Gobi didn't say anything, just pointed in the opposite direction. 'Shower is through there.'

The bathroom was a green marble grotto. My reflection

stared back at me from a full-length mirror, a skinny, pale American kid with a face that looked like two pounds of Genoa sausage. I kicked off my boxers and stepped into the shower. By now my teeth were chattering and it took me a moment to figure out the faucets, but once I did, the shower head rewarded me with an oscillating spray of hot needles that made my whole body realize that it wasn't dead after all. Maybe things weren't as bad as I thought. I breathed in steam, scrubbed myself twice, and stood there until the hot water started to go cold. After what felt like a long time, I stepped out and found a fluffy hotel bathrobe waiting on the back of the door. I was actually starting to feel human again.

'This is a really nice place,' I said, stepping out of the steam. 'How can you afford a place like this?' No answer. 'Gobi?'

A flicker of motion in one of the mirrors. 'Over here.'

'I – oh.'

When she stepped out from behind the closet door, I saw that she'd slipped off the leather jacket. The top underneath it was lacy and black, with shiny thin straps that stretched across her clavicles.

'What are you looking at?'

'Just – your clavicles. You have really nice ones.'

'How are you with zippers?'

'Excuse me?'

She turned her back to me, tilted her head forward, and lifted up her hair from the back of her neck. 'It's stuck.'

'I told you I had a girlfriend, right?'

'I am only asking you to do my zipper.'

'Right.' The zipper slipped down easily. 'Don't you want to know what I'm doing in Venice?'

'No.'

'I'm touring with Inchworm, and – '

She turned around and kissed me, mouth open, tongue flicking up and in as her hands slipped into the bathrobe. I could taste the dry fruity flavor of the champagne she'd just been drinking, and something almost bitter, like dark espresso beans or black licorice. From outside I could hear music and faint laughter down the canal. I drew back, catching my breath.

'Her name's Paula,' I said. 'She's really cool. You'd like her.'

A smoky chuckle and she muttered something in Lithuanian.

'What?'

'I called you a stupid ass.'

'Why?'

'Is what you call a man who has a girl in his bed and still makes small talk.'

'We're not in b–'

She pressed her palms against my chest and pushed me backwards onto the mattress, knocking the pillows aside, rolling over the blankets and up against the headboard, where I was pinned as she straddled me.

'Okay, look, this isn't cool.' The harder I tried to sit up, the harder she pushed back. 'I don't remember you being so – ' I tried to think of another word for *aggressive,* but all of a sudden my word-finding ability seemed to have taken a serious hit to the word-place, whatever it was called. Randomly I noticed a Louis Vuitton steamer trunk in the corner of the room that looked like it cost about a million dollars, and then Gobi shifted her hips slightly on top of me and I forgot all about the steamer trunk and the million dollars it must have cost.

'Are you all right?' she asked.

'I'm fine . . . ?' My voice went up at the end, sounding

like one of the Chipmunks. I put my hands behind me and tried to pull myself free, but her knees had pinned the bathrobe to the mattress. 'I'm just kinda naked under this thing?'

'Perry.'

'What?'

'I need your help.'

I looked into her eyes. 'You need *me?*'

'I am not joking.'

'Sure,' I said, 'whatever I can do.'

And then the Louis Vuitton trunk started to move.

'Run (I'm a Natural Disaster)' – Gnarls Barkley

I sat up fast, looking around so quickly that I felt my neck pop.

'Wait – ' I stared back at the steamer trunk, where something was definitely thumping around inside. 'Is there somebody in that thing?'

Gobi sighed and climbed off me, sliding from the bed in one graceful move. With the resigned air of a woman going about some onerous but necessary task, she opened the drawer of the nightstand next to the bed and pulled out a pistol, screwing the silencer onto the barrel as she walked over to the trunk.

'Wait, what is that? What are you doing?'

Gobi pointed the gun at the steamer trunk and pulled the trigger. The silenced gunshots weren't particularly loud – three metallic champagne corks – and whatever was inside gave a shuddering howl and collapsed to the bottom with a thump. In the frozen moment of realization, I saw smoke drifting out of the bullet holes in the trunk, uncurling like ghostly pigtails in the tastefully recessed lighting.

I floundered off the bed and across the room to my wet pile of clothes, the bathrobe flopping open as I tried to get backwards to the door. Behind me, Gobi's voice was quiet and stern.

'Perry.'

'What?'

'I told you that I need your help.'

'Yeah, well, dead bodies are kind of a deal-breaker for me in that department.'

That was when the pounding started outside the door.

10

'Police and Thieves' – The Clash

'Who is that?' I was standing in the corner by the door, trying to put my jeans back on, but they were too wet and I couldn't even get one foot through the leg hole. I finally just gave up and tied the bathrobe tight around my waist, all too aware that I was naked underneath it. 'What the hell is going on?'

'This way.' Gobi was dragging the trunk away from the wall with one hand, holding the pistol in the other. 'Come on.'

'There's a person in there!'

'Was, yes. Is dead person now.'

'No. No – I'm not – '

Wham-wham-wham! Heavy, authoritative fists hammered louder on the door of the suite, seeming to make the air shake around us. I stumbled forward, my spine suddenly electrified inside me, shooting down from the base of my brain all the way to wherever humans' vestigial tail had dropped off two million years ago. Right now I was ready to dive back into the primordial ooze and take my chances with the single-celled organisms – maybe they had the right idea, staying where they were.

Voices came from outside, angry, urgent – soldiers or cops, it sounded like, shouting in Italian.

'Oh, shit, who's that?'

'Carabinieri, probably.'

'Carbon who?'

'I will explain to you later if we are still alive,' she said. 'Right now, you need to . . . How do you say it? Hold up your end?'

BANG! BANG! BANG! More angry voices, giving orders, making demands in voices that sounded more and more like Mussolini's Blackshirts on a bender.

'What am I supposed to do?'

She hoisted the steamer trunk by one of its straps,

dragging it toward the balcony. 'Lift. Now.'

'What? Why?'

She gestured over the balcony, down to the canal.

'Oh, no. No way. No.'

'We must get rid of the body before . . .' She nodded at the door where the knocking and the shouting had fallen abruptly, ominously silent.

'Forget it!'

She pointed the pistol at me. 'It was good to see you again, Perry.'

'Wait, hold on. I'm not getting involved in this.'

'Already you are involved.'

Click. Safety off. Argument over. I gripped the leather strap and hoisted up my end of the trunk. As I lifted, I felt something inside do a slumping barrel roll over to my end, which got suddenly heavier, and we heaved it up onto the balcony, balancing it on the wrought-iron railing. For just a second I looked down, four stories, where the Grand Canal shimmered below in the darkness, jewels of light reflected from the hotels and buildings on the other side. Venice never looks lovelier than when you're using it to dispose of a body.

Then Gobi shoved the trunk over the edge and it fell.

There was a long silence followed by a splash below just as the hotel door swung open behind us. When I looked back at Gobi, she was already climbing over the railing into the night.

'What are you doing?'

She let go of the railing and disappeared.

11

'Jump' – Van Halen

My decision to go over the railing was pure hot-stove reflex, not involving much in the way of rational thought. It was more like a series of images, bold and simple – Kabuki risk assessment, not recommended to anyone who might ever need to justify their actions afterward to the authorities.

From the other side of the suite, I saw men pouring through the open door – they wore black long-sleeved T-shirts and black pants, and carried automatic weapons, machine pistols, heavy artillery. If these guys were cops, then Venice had a serious paramilitary budget. I could still see the copper wires dangling from the key-slot where they'd disabled the electronic lock.

The man in front looked straight at me, his face instantly familiar. Unlike the others, he was wearing a suit.

So you found it.

Your little tourist trap.

The next thing I knew, I was over the railing, the hotel bathrobe billowing out around my bare legs in the chill night air while my wet toes curled and skidded along the outer rim of the balcony.

The man in front shouted in Italian, swinging his gun up toward me.

I let go.

Spilling back through the open air, pinwheeling my arms in wild, frantic circles as if I might suddenly remember how to fly, I seemed to fall for a long, long time – long enough to think, *I left my bass up there,* and then, *This is really going to hurt* – while they kept yelling at me from up above.

And then pain, which is basically the same in any language. The water flattened me, punching the air out of my lungs – I swear for a second I actually *bounced.* Then my legs went numb, seemed almost to disappear, and I may have blacked out.

The water around me was freezing, squid-ink black, and

I was thrashing around, wondering if anything was broken and guessing it probably wasn't if I was swimming. But I couldn't breathe. When I did, things started to make a little more sense.

The steamer trunk had bobbed to the surface in front of me, kind of swaying up and down in the water. The latch had burst open on impact. I felt a hand brush past my arm. I took it blindly, pulling hard.

'Perry!'

Gobi's voice drifted from somewhere off in the distance. It didn't occur to me to wonder how she could be so far away when I had her arm right here.

I pulled harder on the arm, clamping on to it with both hands, and that was when a man's body floated out of the trunk and straight at me. He was older, bald, dressed in black, wearing a white priest's collar, which had come loose when he'd hit the water and now stuck out on one side. His lips gawped, water from the canal washing in and out of his mouth, and then I saw his eyes pop open, and he looked right at me.

'Shit!' That's what I was trying to say – it's certainly what I was thinking, but it probably came out more like

'Aiiiggghhghh!' I shoved back from him, flailing my arms in the water. 'Oh shit, *shit!*' I tried to say, but this time all that emerged was a spew of bubbles. *Glubb-blitt-bripp.*

'Perry!'

Now Gobi sounded worried. Gunfire rattled from overhead – a series of flat, popping cracks like somebody snapping rolls of the world's deadliest bubble wrap – hitting the water like hail, splashing it up around me. When I looked up I saw two men on the balcony. Gaudy bouquets of orange and yellow muzzle-flash splattered around them.

I flung my arms out and started flurrying them hard in the direction of Gobi's voice, paddling like hell for the stone bridge in front of me. At least it was dark under there. Grabbing a deep breath, I plunged low and kicked as hard as I could.

The sudden roar of a diesel engine filled the space beneath the bridge, above and below the surface, overtaking everything. I bobbed up to see the low white hull of the vaporetto closing in over me, too fast to dodge. I slapped the bow, tried to push myself off, and felt something grab the soaked collar of the sopping hotel bathrobe that clung to my bare skin, hoisting me out of the water to land hard on the deck. An abrupt bundle of dry fabric fell over my head.

Gobi's eyes flashed from the shadows like a pair of unaffordable earrings in a darkened jeweler's window.

'Hold still.'

'You . . .'

'Shut up.'

'. . . *shot* . . .'

'Are you deaf?'

'. . . a *priest*?'

Gobi reached up and clapped her hand over my mouth. I realized she'd wrapped a trench coat over my soaking wet bathrobe.

'Keep your head low.'

'You're insane.'

She didn't argue. I wondered where she'd gotten the dry trench coat and decided not to ask – it probably meant there was some tourist on the boat sprawled out unconscious or worse. The vaporetto lurched forward, spewing diesel fumes, its engines roaring behind us as it nosed its way toward the next stop. When it hit the shore, I could already hear the two-note European sirens dopplering up the canal, blue

71

lights flashing from a police boat headed in the opposite direction, the night waking up around us.

'This is our stop.' She put her arm around me, pulling me upward, jostling me down the floating platform.

'Forget it, I'm done.'

'Idiot.' Nobody did exasperation like she did – you'd think she'd invented it. Tilting slightly to one side, she cocked her right leg, simultaneously sweeping her right hand back, and when it reappeared I saw the knife, six inches long and flickering brightly in all that remained of the light. 'No more Perry Stormaire bullshit.' She pronounced it *bool-sheet*.

'Wait,' I said, 'now there's a type of bullshit named after me?'

'Come now.'

'Or what, you'll cut my throat?'

'Not necessary.' She considered. 'Maybe I just sever Achilles tendon and leave you here helpless in the alley for whatever comes along.' I didn't like the sound of that any more than the sirens that were warbling from up the canal. 'Those police, they are not the only ones looking for a stupid American boy tonight, you know.'

'Those guys back in your hotel room were the same ones who beat me up in the alley outside Harry's.'

'They followed us.'

I flashed on the body floating out of the steamer trunk. 'You shot a priest.'

'Monash?' She shook her head and made a noise like 'pah.' 'Was no priest.'

'He sure looked like one to me.'

'Yes, and once upon a time you thought I was just a foreign exchange student.'

'What's your point?'

'You should learn to use your eyes.'

'I was actually too preoccupied trying not to drown.'

'There is more work to do.'

'Oh, no. No more. No way.'

'You should know better,' Gobi said, and kept the knife where I could see it. 'With me it is never just one.'

12

'Here I Go Again' – Whitesnake

'He's not dead, you know.'

Gobi stopped walking. She'd been leading me down a narrow cobblestone walkway, through an arched gate between two high stone buildings that looked half a millennium old – although 'leading' is probably too gentle a word when you've got a knife wedged tight against your ribs, close enough that its tip keeps jabbing you through a wet hotel bathrobe.

'What are you saying?'

'That guy in the water,' I said. 'Monash, or whatever his name was? I saw him open his eyes.'

'Was reflex. I shot five times.'

'Three.'

'What?'

'You shot him three times.' I could still hear the shots in my head. 'One, two, three.'

'I had already shot him twice before I even put him in trunk. Is no way he could still be alive.'

'Whatever,' I said. 'Just let me go. It's not like I'm going to be able to drive you around Venice in a gondola to kill more people. I can't even water-ski.'

She didn't say anything.

'How did you find me, anyway?'

'Website for your band, what is it? Itch-worm?'

'*Inch*worm.'

'Your tour schedule is posted online.'

'You were stalking me?'

She rolled her eyes. 'Perry, please. Do not flatten yourself.'

'Flat*ter*,' I said. 'Is it possible your English is actually getting worse?'

'I have a friend at Harry's. I gave him your picture and told him to call me when you turned up.'

'*When* I turned up . . . ?' I stared at her. 'Now who's flattening themselves?'

She gave me a look, half smile, half head shake, like I'd simultaneously amused and disappointed her.

'What,' I said, 'you think I couldn't help myself? I was supposed to go straight to the hotel with the rest of the band.'

'Yet you did not.'

'I got lost. I needed somewhere to dry off.'

'You were hoping that I would be there. Admit it.'

'No, I – ' What was the point of arguing? Gobi glanced up, and when I saw a slight smile on her face, I realized that in some perverse way she was enjoying this.

'Perry. This is good.'

'Yeah, it's awesome.'

'We work well together, I think – a good team, yes?'

'Great.' We had stopped in front of a towering old church, its cathedral rising up into the night. 'How many more priests do you have to kill?'

'I told you, he was not a real priest.'

'All right, how many more guys?'

'Only two.'

'Are you sure about that?'

Ignored. Turning away from the church, we followed the shadows around the open piazza, turning right down an even narrower alley. A lit sign ahead hung in the darkness, the curved letters spelling out TRATTORIA SACRO E PROFANO. Even with my nonexistent Italian I could figure that one out: the Trattoria of the Sacred and the Profane.

Gobi stopped and looked over her shoulder in the direction of the church, then back at the front of the restaurant. With its stone façade and pillars flanking the entrance, the café almost looked like a cathedral in miniature. A cigarette vending machine stood just outside the door, gleaming softly in the rain.

'Do you even know where we are?' I whispered.

She didn't say anything. I thought about New York, when she'd had the BlackBerry with its maps and built-in GPS, none of which we had now. Up till this moment I'd assumed she was familiar with Venice, but suddenly she didn't seem so sure of herself.

'Wait, are we lost?'

She stared at me blankly, and for a second it was as if she didn't recognize me at all. That was when I noticed something under her nose, a dark spot trickling downward over her upper lip.

'You're bleeding,' I said. Which was odd, given that nobody had attacked us in the last ten minutes. Gobi touched her finger to her upper lip, then wiped it on her jacket.

'Is nothing.' But she sounded a little dazed and distant, not herself at all, and when she looked at me again it still was almost as if she didn't know who I was.

I had seen her like this before, back in New York. When she'd come to live with my family as a foreign exchange student, back when I thought that's all she was, she'd told us she had epilepsy – it had prevented her from learning to drive, and every so often she had seizures. Not the big, twitching, swallow-your-tongue kind, but more like blackouts. For a second I thought she was going to black out on me now, go into one of her petit mals.

But she's never bled like that before, a voice murmured inside my head. That was new. I was pretty sure that epilepsy didn't give you nosebleeds.

It didn't matter. My legs tensed. If she went into one of her spells, I was definitely making a break for it.

But Gobi just dabbed the rest of the blood away with the back of her hand, grabbed the door handle, and hustled me into the Trattoria of the Sacred and the Profane.

13

'Church of the Poison Mind' – Culture Club

Inside, I smelled sawdust and wet marble, like the basement of a Renaissance cathedral. Shadowy figures huddled at the tables, sipping wine by candlelight – locals or lost tourists, I assumed, at this hour of the night. The only touch of modernity was the unattended video slot machine next to the door with a handwritten sign on it that probably said OUT OF ORDER.

'Stay still,' Gobi said, and started walking toward the bar. She sounded like her usual self again. My eyes had just started to adjust to this deeper, subterranean darkness. I looked again at the figures seated around us, and when I saw who they were, I felt a cold, rubber-gloved hand of dread tightening over my stomach.

The whole room was full of priests.

I went over to the bar, getting as close as I could to Gobi, leaning forward to whisper in her ear. 'What are you doing? We're in a *priest bar.*'

'Do not lose your nerve on me, Perry.' She spoke without turning her head, without seeming to move her lips. 'Just turn around slowly and wait.'

I did as she said, trying to figure how long it would take me to run back out the door. The priests sat at their tables, gathered here in near silence like a murder of crows. Fat ones, skinny ones, old ones, young ones – they must have come here from the cathedral across the piazza. Was this where they hung out after mass? At first count I guessed there were eight or ten of them eating or murmuring to one another, sipping a glass of wine or reading the newspaper, candlelight glinting off their spectacles. Several of them had already taken notice of our arrival, and without staring, I tried to guess which of them wasn't the real priest, which one wasn't going to be walking out of here tonight. I felt the irrational urge to shout at them: *Why aren't you in church?*

There was a flicker of movement in my peripheral vision.

Behind the bar, a woman reached down and brought out a long cardboard box, like the kind you'd use to deliver long-stemmed roses, and laid it on the counter with a muffled but somehow very loud thump.

Gobi picked up the box, weighed it in her hands, and nodded. I saw her hand reappear holding a plastic bag filled with rolls of carefully bundled euros, which she placed on the counter. The woman on the other side made it disappear so quickly that it was almost like it had never been there. The entire transaction took less than three seconds. My heart was pounding hard, and I was pretty sure that I could make it to the front door in three steps.

That was when the police walked in.

14

'The World Has Turned and Left Me Here'
– Weezer

It must have been sheer luck. As soon as the cops stepped through the doorway in their dark blue uniforms and berets, laughing and talking to each other, I knew they hadn't come here looking for us. They weren't the same ones from the hotel, and their relaxed, casual banter told me that they were on routine patrol and had just happened to walk into the wrong place at the wrong time.

Like I said, pure luck – all bad.

They stopped and stared at us, and I knew that there had to be some kind of official bulletin already circulating from what happened at the hotel, with our physical descriptions.

One female, armed and dangerous, dressed in black; one male, scared and wet, dressed in terrycloth.

'Okay, listen.' I put up my hands. 'I'm not part of this. I'll go quietly, okay?'

Slightly behind me and off to my left, Gobi flipped open the box that the woman behind the bar had given her and took out a sawn-off shotgun, swinging it upward in one unhesitating move. At the sight of the gun, both cops – carabinieri, she'd called them, the Italian 5-0 – dropped instantly into defensive stances on the other side of the doorway, going for their own sidearms, as Gobi pumped a round into the shotgun and pointed the barrel right up under my chin.

'What are you doing?' I muttered.

The cops started shouting at us, both of them at once. Their voices sounded booming and authoritative in the confined space of the trattoria. Gobi didn't answer, just kept the barrel where it was, pointed up at my head, where twelve years of education were waiting to become paint on the ceiling. Her eyes were locked on the officers blocking the door. On either side, the priests were staring at us with unblinking, owlish eyes. Last rites, anyone?

'*Allontanare,*' Gobi said, in what sounded like perfect Italian. Her eyes were locked on the cops. '*Ottenga indietro o muore.*'

The carabinieri stared at her. Their faces changed and all the bravado and adrenaline drained away from their cheeks. Slowly, they lowered their guns and stepped away from the door.

'What did you tell them?'

'I said if they moved, I would kill you.'

'That's it? They looked terrified.'

'They saw that I meant it.'

Gobi nudged me through the door. Then, turning around, she braced her back against one of the stone pillars that stood outside the entrance, doubled up her legs, and used her feet to shove the cigarette machine over so it landed on its side in front of the doorway with a crash. She spun me around and we started hustling back across the piazza, my bare feet stumbling numbly over cobblestones.

'Where are you staying?' she asked.

'What?'

'What is your hotel?'

'*My* hotel? You want to go to –'

87

'We cannot very well go back to where I was staying, can we?'

'I can't – ' I shook my head as if to connect a few of the disconnected thought-Legos rattling around inside. 'I don't remember.'

'We need to disappear for a little while. Somewhere quiet.'

'How about Connecticut?'

Almost on cue, loud voices came spilling through the open piazza, sounding drunk and unruly. A group of twenty-something Americans were stumbling toward us, coming back from some bar, yelling and laughing.

'Hey, dude!' one of them shouted, pumping his fist in the air. 'Viva la Resistance!'

'We need to get off the streets right now,' Gobi said. 'Otherwise there is only death for us here.'

'So none of those priests back there was your target?'

'That was simply a weapons buy,' she said with a shrug, 'nothing more. I have one more target here in Venice, but first we must cool off.' The shotgun touched my lower spine. 'Where is your hotel?'

I closed my eyes and tried to think of the place that

Norrie had mentioned over the phone. The name popped into my head. Thank you, high school study skills. 'Guerrato,' I said, 'something like that. Pensione Guerrato? By the Rialto Bridge?'

On the far side of the piazza, behind the church, Gobi stopped in front of a Telecom Italia phone, grabbed the receiver, and pushed me down into the shadows while she called what I assumed was the operator. I heard her murmuring in Italian. When she pulled me back up, we were already moving again, over the biggest stone bridge yet, overlooking the dark canal and closed windows, expensive galleries and shops of luxuries, none of which were as appealing as the prospect of just getting out of here alive.

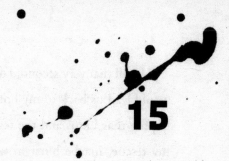

15

'Happiness Is a Warm Gun' – The Beatles

'Hold it.'

It was just a whisper. We were in a square along one of the canals, sometime after one a.m. Greenish-black water lapped up in every doorway and stairwell. I stopped, Gobi's hand on my shoulder, and saw that she was staring across the tiny square, past a row of pushcarts that had been covered for the night, down a narrow street off to our right.

'What?'

She didn't answer. A second later she moved, cutting across the square, leaving me standing there alone in the moonlight.

I need to get out of here, I thought.

Up till that very second, I'd somehow assumed that Gobi would lead us back to my hotel and I'd start making noise, hoping that Linus and the rest of the band would come to my rescue, maybe burst in with an arsenal of guitars and microphones and distract her with a few verses of 'All the Young Dudes' while I phoned the authorities. Now, though, I realized that this would just put them in harm's way. This tour was over. In our current situation, showing up with Gobi was the equivalent of rolling a live grenade down the aisle of a Boeing 747. You couldn't escape her; you could only hope to survive her.

I needed to run, to get far away. Maybe I could get a job on a fishing boat and sail down to Capri, start a bar on the beach and wear rope-soled sandals, and send a message summoning the rest of the band down to join me when the coast was clear.

I turned and started sprinting in the opposite direction, trying to calculate the least visible trajectory. From behind me I heard an object rattle off the stone, clattering.

Something big and smelly slammed into me from behind, hard enough to knock me off my feet. It was like being hit by a roll of remnant carpeting. I tumbled forward and caught myself, scraping my palms, and looked around to see a thickly bearded guy in a heavy woolen overcoat sprawled on his side next to me, clutching his head and groaning. The gash on his face was trickling blood, and he was trying to get up, cursing in what sounded like German or Arabic or Russian, one of those great guttural languages full of surliness and phlegm.

Gobi seemed to recognize him at once. 'Swierczynski.' Her boot came down hard on the guy's chest, pinning him to the concrete. 'Do not move.' When I sat up, I saw that she had the shotgun pointed at his head, but he and I were lying close enough that she could have just as easily had it pointed at me. 'Open your coat.'

The guy, Swierczynski, muttered something in his own language.

'Open now.' Gobi reached down and ripped the coat open, exposing a camera with an expensive-looking telephoto lens hanging from a strap around his neck. She scowled at the camera like she'd expected nothing less.

'Are you working for Kaya now?' she asked.

The guy glared at her, then gave a grudging nod.

'Tell Kaya that I do not need a nursemaid.' She yanked

the camera loose from his grasp, then searched his other pockets, pulling out a switchblade, a cell phone, and a thick roll of euros and pocketing all of that as well. 'Tell him I do the job as arranged.'

Swierczynski nodded again.

'Tell him the next tail he puts on me, I send back to him in pieces. Can you remember all this, or you need me to carve it on your chest?'

'Stupid cow.' The man spat blood in her direction. The accent was eastern European, maybe Polish. 'I am not idiot.'

'Sometimes people forget things after they hit their head.'

He sneered. 'You didn't hit me that hard.'

'Not yet.' Gobi turned and glanced back at me. 'Hit him.'

'Me?'

'Is time you learned to fight.'

'No.'

She turned and aimed the shotgun at him again. 'Do it, or I finish him off now.'

'Okay, seriously – '

'Make a fist.'

'I know how to throw a punch.' I looked at the man with the beard, standing there waiting for me to hit him.

'Stand with feet apart at shoulder width,' Gobi said, taking the position as she described it. 'Bend your knees. Elbows back, fists here. In kendo, this is horse stance.'

'Look, I really don't –'

Swierczynski went for the shotgun. It wasn't the most agile move in the world, not particularly speedy or graceful, but he did have the element of surprise on his side, and for a second it almost seemed like he was going to get away with it. Then Gobi's right foot lashed out so fast that I almost felt sorry for the guy. I heard the cartilage pop in his knee as she swept his leg from the side and dropped him into a pile on the street.

Gobi picked up the shotgun and leveled it at his head. 'This will be loud.' Her stance was different now, as if she were already preparing for the recoil. 'Get ready.'

Swierczynski lifted his head. 'If you kill me,' he said, in his low, heavily accented English, 'you will die. Kaya will make sure of it.'

Gobi didn't move.

'He told me everything.' His lips twisted into an ugly

grin, and he pointed to his temple. 'He told me the bullet is already in your head.'

Gobi exhaled. Then, without a sound, she lowered the gun, pointing it back at me.

'Walk,' she told me, and we left him lying at the side of the street.

16

'Know Your Enemy' – Green Day

Key questions for discussion at this point:

1. Who's Kaya?
2. Why was the guy following us, trying to take Gobi's picture?
3. How come Gobi was killing guys dressed as priests?
4. 'The bullet is already in your head'? WTF?
5. Who or what did Kaya have that gave him control over Gobi?
6. Was I ever going to get to wear anything more than a stolen overcoat over a wet hotel bathrobe?

7. Was this seriously as good as my time in Venice was going to get? Because if so – dude, major disappointment.

17

'There Are Some Remedies Worse Than the Disease' – This Will Destroy You

Gobi didn't answer any of these questions, of course, just jabbed me from behind to keep me walking. It was kind of this fun language we worked out: I asked a question, she poked me in the spine with the shotgun. Ever since my abortive attempt at escape across the square, the shotgun was pointed at me exclusively again. It made me feel special.

'Is Kaya the one that hired you to kill the guys who aren't priests?'

'Kaya did not hire me.'

'So why are you doing it?'

'I am not a hired killer.'

The shotgun pushed me harder. The sign for the Pensione Guerrato hung on the left-hand side of an alleyway leading from an empty marketplace in the Rialto Mercato. Gobi took one look at the surveillance camera hanging above the door and stepped back.

'You push it.' Hanging back from the doorway, she lowered the shotgun and shoved me toward the brass-plated intercom button. 'Keep your head tilted down.'

I lowered my head, pressed the button, and waited what felt like a long time until a man's voice answered through the speaker. *'Buona sera.'*

'Uh, hello. Do you speak English?'

'Yes.'

'My name is, ah . . .' My mind went blank. '. . . Jim Morrison. I need a room for the night.'

The door buzzed and I opened it. It led into a narrow vestibule of varnished wooden walls and a steep, creaky staircase rising upward into what felt like perilous heights. Gobi's footsteps stayed right behind me the whole time, and I could feel the shotgun ever so slightly against my back, an ugly reminder that we weren't done here.

We got to the top step. The landing was decorated with

antique chairs and statues, lace-draped tables and floor lamps. Bookshelves lined the far wall next to old maps of the city and opera posters. Behind the front desk, a distinguished, GQ-looking guy in his fifties sat next to an iMac flat-screen, holding a cup of tea.

I stepped forward, trying to clutch the trench coat around my neck so it wasn't totally obvious that all I had underneath was a bathrobe. 'I'm Jim.' I cleared my throat. 'This is my friend Gobi.'

'Yes, of course.' The man smiled and Gobi smiled back, clutched my arm, laying her head on my shoulder. In the mirror across the lobby I saw us standing there together and felt a dull sense of amazement. Especially with the camera around Gobi's neck, we looked like two weary travelers at the end of a long day who just wanted to tumble into bed together.

'I am Benito,' the man said. 'It is a pleasure to meet you.' He handed us a big brass key on a tassel. 'You are staying in room fourteen, right up the stairs.'

'Do you have something more private?' Gobi brought out the wad of euros that she'd taken from Swierczynski, peeled off several large bills, and laid them on the counter. 'A suite in another part of the hotel, perhaps?'

Benito's eyes moved over the money. 'Of course, *signora*.' He didn't miss a beat, hanging up the first key and giving us another. 'I am certain that I can accommodate you.'

'We enjoy our privacy.' She peeled off another hundred and slid it across the counter. 'If it is possible, we would appreciate your complete discretion.'

'Absolutely.'

'Thank you,' Gobi said, and took the key, nudging me forward toward the stairs.

•   . ◆ ◗

'You're seriously tying me to the bedposts?' I asked.

'Only arms.' She tightened the thick braided cords that she'd cut from the curtains, checking the knots around my wrists while I lay there with my arms above my head, shivering. With the wet bathrobe off, I'd been reduced to the blankets she'd tossed over me, with nothing underneath. 'I do not want to lose you, Perry.'

'How romantic.'

She shook her head. 'Only you would think so.'

'I can't sleep like this.'

'Try.'

'What happens in the morning when the rest of the guys start tearing this place apart, looking for me?'

'I should be gone by then.'

'Wait, what?'

She switched off the light. A moment later I heard the shower go on. When it stopped, the bathroom door creaked open. I smelled steam and soap, some kind of shampoo and conditioner, and a tiny cell phone screen appeared, the one she'd taken from Swierczynski, floating in the darkness on the far side of the room. I heard her voice murmuring in Lithuanian, soft consonants and *s*-sounds, just above a whisper. It reminded me of when she was living at our house in Connecticut, the way that I'd sometimes heard her talking through the wall. Back then we'd thought she was calling her family in Lithuania. Who was she calling now?

Despite what I'd told her about not being able to sleep with my arms above my head, I must have dozed off, because at some point, I felt her slip in bed next to me, heard the bedsprings creak underneath me. Although our bodies didn't touch, I was aware of the warmth of her skin in the cool sheets and the faint, even sound of her breathing. Her bare arm brushed against mine. I could smell leather and the faint ocean smell mixed with whatever she'd used to wash her hair.

'Gobi?'

'What?'

'I seriously can't feel my arms.'

'I can.' She rolled over and put her hand on my chest. 'Your heart is pounding.'

'Pain elevates the heart rate.'

'Is that really what you want to talk about now?' she said. 'Pain?'

'Don't.' I tried to move away, but the cords around my wrists weren't going anywhere. 'I told you . . .'

Her hand slid over my stomach and farther down. 'You are telling me something very different now.'

'That's – '

'What?'

'. . .'

'. . .'

She let out a chuckle, patted me on the chest and rolled over onto her back. 'Go to sleep,' she said. 'Tomorrow is a busy day.'

18

'Panic Switch' – Silversun Pickups

'Perry?'

I opened my eyes and tried to sit up, then remembered that I couldn't. My shoulders were on fire, and my neck ached like I had iron rods running down from the base of my skull. Off to the right, there was a rattling sound as the heavy curtains swung open and daylight exploded in my face. It was blinding enough that I could barely make out the female silhouette poised in front of it.

'Okay,' I managed, 'we've established that it's morning. Can you please untie me now?'

My eyes adjusted, and I got my first real look at the woman standing over me.

It was Paula.

• ✦ ●

She was standing by the window, wearing the coat that she'd no doubt arrived in, and her briefcase was still in one hand and her suitcase in the other. For a moment, we just stared at each other. I realized that the blankets were pulled down to my waist, just far enough to reveal that I wasn't wearing anything underneath them, and I was now acutely aware of my position on the bed.

'I – I finished early in L.A.' She blinked exactly once. The words were dropping out of her mouth like stale candy falling out of a vending machine, just lying there between us. 'I got on a plane. I wanted to surprise you.'

'Officially surprised.'

'Yeah.' Another word that just lay there. 'Me too.'

'Thank God you're here,' I said. 'Gobi –'

'Gobi?' Her eyebrows went up even higher, if that were possible. 'Gobi is here?'

'Who do you think did this?' I tugged on the cords, as if I needed to draw more attention to the fact that I was still tied to the bedposts. 'Can you cut me loose?'

Paula looked at Gobi's clothes strewn around the room, a blouse on the nightstand, something lacy and red dangling from the doorknob. Some dazed part of me realized that Gobi must have gotten up early and gone shopping, then come back here to change while I lay sound asleep. Couldn't she have at least picked up after herself?

When Paula's eyes returned to me again, they were harder to read. The surprise was gone, and there was something else there instead, a kind of keen, businesslike efficiency, as if she were suddenly seeing this from a completely different set of contact lenses. 'Of course.'

'Paula, wait – '

'I'll be right back. I'm just going to go see if they have anything sharp at the front desk.'

The door closed. I lay there staring at the ceiling for what felt like a very long time, trying to identify various stains. One of them looked like a fish. One looked like a bird. One looked like my future imploding.

I looked at the digital clock on the nightstand and saw that it was somehow already two in the afternoon. If Linus and the band had started searching the hotel for me, they hadn't gotten around to breaking down random doors yet.

Finally Paula came back with a pair of very lethal-looking scissors. She reached over the bed toward my arms. Now she wasn't making eye contact with me at all.

'Hold still.'

'Look,' I said, 'Paula – '

'I'm actually here for a reason.' *Snip-snip.* 'Armitage is flying in this afternoon.' *Snip.* 'He wants to meet you personally before tonight's show.' She finished with the first cord and moved on to the second one. 'So I guess I don't have to ask how the tour's going so far.'

'Stop it,' I said. 'Just listen, okay?'

Snip-snip. 'I'm not upset, Perry, all right? I'm a grownup. I get it.'

'But I haven't told you anything.'

'You don't have to.'

'Hold on – '

'I read what you wrote about her, remember? In your college essay?'

'Okay,' I said, 'but that isn't – '

Snip. 'I should never have sent you to Venice.'

'I'm not – '

Snip. 'I ought to have my head examined.'

'Paula, she's killing people again.'

The scissors froze midsnip, and Paula straightened up and looked at me. 'What?'

'Gobi. She's working for somebody named Kaya. He's got something on her, I don't know what, but he's forcing her to do some new assignment. The targets – one of them was dressed as a priest. She made me help her get rid of the body last night and dump it into the canal from her hotel balcony.'

'You helped her get rid of a *body?*'

'That's what I'm trying to tell you. Last night she bought a shotgun at a restaurant and kept it pointed at my back all the way here. We have to call the police right now, before she gets back.'

Paula cut the last cord and my left hand was free at last. I stretched my arm back, working the pins and needles from my shoulder until the circulation came flooding back. She still hadn't said anything. Looking at her eyes, I could see her mind working fast, evaluating the situation and analyzing her options.

'You said you helped her?' she asked.

'No! I mean, yeah, but – '

'Did anybody see you?'

I thought about our standoff with the carabinieri at the Trattoria Sacro e Profano. 'Well, yeah, but – '

'The police?'

'Yes.'

'And they saw your face.' Paula sighed. 'So you're already an accomplice.'

'What?' I stood up. '*No!* I told you, she had a gun to my – '

'Perry,' Paula said, 'listen to me. I believe you, obviously. But you have to look at it their way. Right now you're just an American kid on a rock-and-roll tour, and the last time they saw you, it was this Bonnie and Clyde shootout with a gun-toting psychopath. An international incident like this can go south fast. Even if there was no video surveillance footage of you, they've probably already sent your Identi-Kit facial composite to Interpol right alongside Gobi's.' She closed her eyes and took a deep breath. 'Before we do anything, you need a lawyer – or the next place you're going to end up is in an Italian jail.'

'Jail?' I felt my stomach lurch downward with a sudden

nauseating heaviness. All at once I couldn't breathe. It was like my lungs had just sort of gotten stage fright and forgotten how to do their job. Every movie I'd ever seen with a guy-ends-up-in-a-foreign-jail-cell plot went through my brain all at once, and I was already wondering how many packs of cigarettes I'd be worth on the open market.

When I finally managed to draw breath, my voice sounded wheezy and faint, like an asthmatic gasping down a clogged garden hose. 'I can't go to jail,' I said. 'My dad – '

'I know.'

'What do we do?'

'For now, we need to get you out of here.'

'And then what?'

Paula frowned. 'It's possible that Armitage can help us.'

I looked at her, allowing myself to feel the faintest spark of hope. 'How?'

'Well, for one thing, he's a billionaire. People like him don't go anywhere without a fleet of attorneys. And for some reason, Stormaire, he's taken a liking to you.' She smiled a little. 'There's no way he'll get Inchworm into the studio for their first album if their bass player and songwriter is rotting in a cell somewhere in Venice, right?'

'So what next?'

'We go somewhere and lie low.' She looked at her watch. 'We've got a little over six hours till we meet him tonight. And then all you have to do is play a gig so amazing that Armitage will do whatever it takes to keep you out of jail.'

'I gotta tell the guys I'm here.'

Paula shook her head. 'No offense to Linus, but at this point the last thing we need is his particular brand of high-pitched rhetoric. We'll deal with him soon enough.'

I saw her point. 'Okay, but – '

'First things first.' Her gaze moved back to me, one eyebrow raised. 'Where are your clothes, anyway?'

'I haven't seen them since last night.'

'You've been naked since yesterday?'

'Except for a hotel bathrobe and a stolen overcoat,' I said, 'yeah.'

'I'll send the desk clerk out with my AmEx.' Paula shook her head, but she was still smiling. 'I have to say, Stormaire, in spite of everything else, when I first saw you tied to the bedposts like that, it got me kind of tingly.'

'I'm glad to hear you say that,' I said. 'Because the way

you looked at me, I thought you might try cutting off something different.'

'Are you kidding? After waiting this long? I'd probably miss it more than you would.'

'I doubt that.'

She smiled, then folded up that smile and put it away, all business, all at once. It was uncanny how she could do that, but I couldn't imagine not having her on my side.

'Can I ask one more question?'

Paula glanced up. 'What?'

'How did *you* figure out what room I was in?'

'You checked in under the name Jim Morrison, Perry. You might as well have hung out a freaking sign.'

'I guess.'

'Now come on,' she said, and gave me a lascivious glance. 'Let's get you some clothes before I lose what's left of my willpower.'

19

'Busy Child' – The Crystal Method

In a city like Venice, most of the nicer hotels claim to have been palaces at one time or another. But there were palaces and there were *palaces,* and the Gritti, where Paula said we had a room, was a silk-draped, marble-floored, gold-rimmed old-world marvel that didn't exactly go along with what I imagined when I thought about lying low. The kid staring back at me in the lobby mirrors didn't look like he belonged here, but then, at that moment, he didn't look like he necessarily belonged anywhere.

'You can afford this?' I murmured, gazing across the mostly empty lobby.

'Armitage keeps a suite here.'

'Is he here now?'

'He'll meet us later for dinner. Just relax, all right? Go stand by the elevators and wait for me.'

Paula went to check in while I hovered behind a pillar, trying to look inconspicuous. I was wearing skinny European jeans and a Venice T-shirt with a baseball cap and sunglasses. I had a garment bag over my shoulder, the one that Benito, the desk clerk at the Pensione Guerrato, had brought back for me before we'd slipped out.

When Paula came back with the key, we took the elevator up to Armitage's suite, and I gazed out on the Grand Canal and the city beyond, trying not to think about how less than twenty-four hours ago, I'd been trying to get rid of a corpse from a similar height.

'You like the view?'

'It's great.'

'Perry . . .'

I looked around. Paula was sitting on the bed, gazing at me in a way that I'd never seen before.

'We've still got a few hours to kill,' she said. 'Any ideas?'

'We could send down for some champagne.'

'That sounds like a good start, but where do we go from there?'

I sat down next to her on the bed and we started kissing. Paula slipped her hand inside my T-shirt, and we sprawled backwards over the covers, and all I could think was *This is it. You're in Europe now, you're alone in a hotel room, you can do whatever you want.* I thought about how most guys, including my friends, had lost their virginity in the back seat of a car or on their girlfriend's couch, hoping like hell that her dad didn't come down and catch them. Compared to that, this was a dream.

Paula sat up and looked at me. 'What's wrong?'

'Nothing,' I said.

'You seem distracted.'

'No, I'm totally fine, really.'

'I knew it.' Her eyes didn't budge from mine. 'It's her, isn't it?'

'What?' I shook my head. 'Who, Gobi? Are you kidding?'

'I'm not stupid, Perry.'

'Wait,' I said, and grabbed her by the arm, 'just listen to me, okay?'

She just sat there staring at me.

'I'm telling you,' I said. 'There's no one else I'd rather be here with right now. No one.'

Paula kept her eyes on me, her expression unchanged. Somewhere down in the piazza, a church bell rang. She took a breath.

'Prove it.'

‘Perry, you ready yet? It's time.'

'One second.' It was almost six o'clock now, and I was still in the bathroom, trying to fix my tie. 'I'll be right there.'

'Perry, we have to go.'

'All right.' Taking a big breath, I turned the knob and stepped out of the bathroom. 'I'm ready, let's go.'

Paula didn't say anything right away. She got an odd look on her face, a kind of half frown, half pucker that I'd never seen before, and bit the corner of her lip. The European-style suit that Benito at the front desk had brought back fit me well enough – in fact, it almost fit too well, the narrow, tapered pants and suit jacket clinging perfectly to my frame in straight, smooth lines. The shirt was made out of some flimsy, silky material that felt like it might dissolve if it got wet, and the lines of the tie were crisp and sharp. My narrow black leather shoes gleamed like mirrors. Somewhere in the universe, every guy that I'd ever hung out with and watched *RoboCop* was asking if I'd like a glass of chardonnay to go with my *Celine Dion Greatest Hits* CD.

'You look . . . great,' she said. 'I've just never seen you like this before. I sort of want to devour you.'

'Still?'

'Again.'

'Now?'

'Always.'

'Oh,' I said. 'Well, thanks. You're looking pretty edible yourself.'

'I packed in a hurry.' Apparently 'in a hurry' meant an extremely low-cut black cocktail dress with a stylized zipper running diagonally down the front, a white cropped fur coat, and stilettos that probably could have doubled as projectile weapons. I had definitely spent too much time with Gobi, I thought – now I was viewing fashion accessories with the eye of a Secret Service agent. Her hair was pinned up, accentuating her throat and ears, where she wore no jewelry whatsoever. Something about that tan, uninterrupted skin made me want to kiss it, which I'm sure was the whole point.

'Don't forget your hat and sunglasses.' She offered her arm. 'Shall we go?'

We took the elevator down, both of us watching the numbers. She reached over and put her hand on my chest.

'How do you feel?'

'Good.'

'Are you sure?'

'I'm positive.'

She turned to me and smiled. If you had told me a year before that day that I would spend several hours up in a luxury hotel room with a beautiful woman and I'd somehow still emerged from the whole thing a virgin, I think I would have skipped over disbelief completely and gone straight to exasperation. But that was how it had happened. Even as we'd wrestled half naked across the sheets, Paula had managed to keep her cool.

It's all right, Perry, she'd said. *I don't want you rushing into*

anything you're not ready for, especially if you're just trying to
prove a point.

I almost asked her what point she thought I was trying to prove, then realized I already knew.

I guess in the end, we both did.

20

'Darklands' – The Jesus and Mary Chain

We walked across the Piazza San Marco, making our way among the pushcarts selling masks and T-shirts to tourists in the gathering dusk. My new shoes felt tight on my feet. Pigeons fluttered and dive-bombed our heads, close enough that I almost had to duck to avoid being hit, and as we walked past the cathedral, I pointed up to the clock tower, where two bronze men swung their clappers to mark the hour.

'Those mechanized figures are called the Moors,' I said, remembering something from a guidebook I'd read on the train here. 'Supposedly back in the seventeenth century one of them knocked an unsuspecting worker off the top and he fell to his death. The first official assassination by a robot.'

That got a smile out of Paula. 'You're a good tour guide, Stormaire. Maybe if this whole rock-and-roll thing doesn't pan out . . .'

'You think Armitage will actually be able to help me sort this out?'

'We'll see.'

I took a deep breath. She glanced across the piazza and I caught the faraway look in her eyes that I hadn't seen before.

'Hey,' I said. 'Are you all right?'

'I have a picture of me sitting on my dad's shoulders right over there.' Paula pointed back to the cathedral, next to the folded-up platforms they kept in the square in times of *acqua alta,* high water, when the canals flooded into the streets. 'I was probably five or six at the time.'

'I didn't know you'd been here before.'

'Dad was here with the Stones back in the early nineties. He brought me with him. It was a good time.'

Her melancholy tone caught me off-guard. 'You guys still see each other all the time, right?'

'Things are different now.' She tugged my hand. 'Come on. We're going to be late.'

We stopped outside a bistro with outdoor tables set up along the cobblestones. As we approached, I saw Linus pacing back and forth in front of the entrance, smoking a cigarette hard enough that it seemed to disappear in two long drags. He saw me and tossed the butt aside.

'Perry, thank God, where have you been?' His attention immediately snapped to Paula. 'What did you do with him?'

Paula sighed. 'Good to see you too, Linus. Where's the rest of the band?'

'They're inside already, doing the sound check. Which is where he should be, right now.'

I hustled inside and found Norrie, Sasha, and Caleb setting up equipment onstage. Caleb was eating an enormous slice of pizza while Sasha flirted with a strikingly beautiful waitress in a language that seemed to rely on nothing more sophisticated than hand gestures and smiles. None of them seemed particularly concerned about my disappearance. 'What's up, jerkweed,' Sasha said. 'What happened? We thought you drowned in a canal or something.'

Norrie squinted at me suspiciously, and when he got close

enough, he lowered his voice and whispered, 'Wuh-Well?'

'Well, what?'

'You nuh-know what, Stormaire. Duh-Did you fuh-find her or what?'

'Dude . . .'

'Yuh-You totally did, didn't you?' He shook his head. 'Thuh-That's why you duh-ditched us.'

'. . . it's a crazy, long story, and – '

'Nuh-Never mind. Doesn't muh-matter. Guh-Guess what?' When he looked at me again, he was smiling, and just like that, his stutter was gone. 'I wrote a new song.'

'Yeah?'

'Yeah. And it's good. All it needs is a bass line.'

'No problem, man.' In spite of everything, I felt that sudden lift that came with our songwriting partnership, that sense that somehow we'd lucked into knowing each other, way back before either one of us could've guessed what that meant. 'Bass line, I can do.'

'Wuh-Wait a second.' Norrie's eyes narrowed. 'Wuh-Where's your bass?'

'I kind of . . . lost it.'

'*What?*'

'Look,' I said, 'if I told you half the shit that I've been through in the last twenty-four hours . . .'

'That's all right,' a voice said. 'I'm sure we can figure something out.'

I turned round and saw George Armitage standing there.

• . ◆ .. ●

In person, Armitage was exactly as refined and charming as I'd imagined from talking to him over the phone. He was in his mid-fifties, tall and fit, his skin almost Mediterranean, with just a few artfully arranged wrinkles around his pale blue eyes. Everything about him felt polished and real at the same time, and there was a certain smell, like suede and Lear jet fumes, clinging ever so faintly to his clothes. *So this is what a billion dollars smells like,* I thought.

The bodyguards on either side of him stood silent, their eyes hidden behind sleek, mirrored sunglasses. I almost immediately started thinking of them as Ram and Rod.

After a brief introduction to the rest of the band, and to Linus, who for once seemed able to keep from making some kind of acerbic comment, Armitage led Paula and me across the square to the small café, where a table was waiting for us. Ram and Rod followed at a respectful but conspicuous distance.

'I won't keep you long,' Armitage said. 'I know you've got a sound check to get to.'

'It's all right.'

'How do you like the city?' He spread his hands magisterially across the café, the cathedral, and the piazza full of pigeons behind us in the gathering dusk, as if he'd conjured all of this out of the ether, just for us. 'My absolute favorite place on earth. She's like a beautiful woman whose favor I've never quite managed to capture.'

'It's really great,' I said.

'I think we should celebrate.' He signaled the waiter. 'Villa Antinori, 'ninety-five.'

The waiter disappeared, and Armitage turned the full wattage of his attention on me. 'Perry, I realize all of this must feel like it's happening very quickly to you, but by now you know how much I love your music, and I think it's time we discuss Inchworm's first album.'

'Okay.'

'I'd like to get you in the studio as soon as this tour is

over, if possible. In fact, we were talking about going directly to L.A. You blokes could certainly recuperate there, and when the time is right, we could start recording right away. How does that sound?'

'Like a dream come true.'

'Wonderful.' Armitage smiled and glanced at Paula. 'Make a note to book some time at Sunset Sound, love, won't you?'

'Taking care of it now,' Paula said. She took her iPad out of her purse and started typing something onto the screen.

The wine arrived, and Armitage poured a glass for each of us.

'That settles it, then,' he said, raising a toast. 'Here's to Inchworm and the great future that awaits them.'

I reached for my glass, and that was when I saw Gobi coming through the crowd, walking straight toward us with the shotgun.

21

'Sweetest Kill' – Broken Social Scene

When I think back on that moment, I'm always amazed by how long it took me to react. Everyone else seemed to move before I did – Paula, the waiters, even the other patrons of the café.

Gobi took out the bodyguards from twenty feet away. I heard two quick, deafening noises – *BLAM, BLAM* – and saw them both pitch backwards in opposite directions, hitting the cobblestones on either side of the table. What I saw then couldn't possibly be right – it had to be some kind of run-time glitch in the mainframe of the universe – because when I looked again, Gobi was less than a foot away, pumping another round into the chamber and pointing the

133

shotgun right at Armitage's chest, point blank.

Armitage opened his mouth to say something, but he never got the chance before Gobi pulled the trigger. There was a third deafening *KAPOW,* and the shotgun blast blew him backwards out of his chair hard enough to knock the whole table over with his knees, spilling wine and glass everywhere. Pigeons took flight and people screamed in that far-off way that voices sound after your eardrums have been assaulted by blunt-force audio trauma. My ears were used to it from years of speakers and amps, and it was still a backwards-sounding scream – the crowd almost seemed to suck it back inward – withering into a gasp, when they saw what had happened.

When I looked down again, Armitage was sprawled backwards on the pavement between his bodyguards, motionless in a huge and still expanding splatter pattern of his own blood. It spread out around him in all directions like the shadow of an object falling fast.

Without hesitating, Gobi reached down with her free hand and grabbed Armitage's body, clutching his sagging weight under the arms, hoisting it up as if it were weightless, holding it in front of herself like a shield, all the while keeping the shotgun in her right hand. There was a distant *CRACK* and I saw another bullet hit the corpse in the chest. Looking around, I realized that the shot had come from somewhere far overhead, and that was when I realized there was at least one other person on a rooftop overhead, shooting down at us.

Gobi raised the shotgun one-handed and fired again, up at the top of the cathedral.

'Stand down.' Somewhere off to my right I saw Paula rise to her feet. I was expecting her to get out a phone to call the cops or an ambulance.

What came out instead was a pistol – polished, nickel-plated, and held with an expert two-handed shooting grip.

And pointed at me.

'Paula?' I asked.

Paula's eyes stayed on Gobi. Her voice was absolutely calm. 'That's a Mossberg pump-action, isn't it? Twelve-gauge, right? Nice gun.'

Gobi didn't say anything.

'Only problem is, you've got to reload before you can shoot again. Move and he dies.'

In front of us, in front of the overturned table, Gobi

stood frozen, still cradling the shotgun in one hand and Armitage's corpse in the other. Even with my ears still ringing, Paula's voice was crisp and totally clear, every syllable chiseled into the air. The realization came slanting at me sideways like a sudden cold rain.

My.

Girlfriend.

Paula.

Was.

Pointing.

A.

Gun.

At.

Me.

I stared at her. I couldn't speak. Couldn't breathe. Still.

In front of us, all at once Gobi chucked the shotgun, shoved Armitage's body away from her, swiveled, and threw her leg straight up into the air, bringing it down in an ax-kick to Paula's face. There was a *crack* and Paula went hard to the ground. Gobi grabbed her iPad, but Paula must not have dropped the gun, because through all the broken glass and blood and wine, she was already firing at us. I should know. I felt at least one of the bullets whining past my head.

My eyes rolled sideways in their sockets like overheated ball bearings, taking in everything at once. From the club across the square, I saw Linus and Norrie come running out. They took one look at what was happening and hit the ground.

That was when Gobi grabbed my arm, manacle-tight, a grip that I now knew exclusively accompanied those moments when it was either run or get shot. If I hadn't run – if she'd still had a gun with live ammo – I think she would have threatened to shoot me herself.

'Go!'

She jerked me forward, swinging me when I wasn't able to keep up. My feet were definitely not in charge – they were just trying to keep me from falling face-first onto the pavement – and we cut across the piazza back in the direction of the cathedral. Vendors and tourists with no idea what was going on turned to watch us go sprinting across between the pushcarts toward a row of gondolas lined up along the water.

Up in the cathedral, bells started clanging through the

square like God's own security system. Somehow I still heard bullets caroming off the pavement behind us. They seemed to be coming from every direction at once, from up above and behind us. I felt my mind split cleanly in half, each side entertaining contradictory thoughts. On one side Armitage was still alive and I was sitting at the café with Paula, listening to him tell me what a genius I was. On the other side, the woman that I thought I had fallen in love with was trying to kill me.

I was beginning to detect a pattern here.

Then we ran out of pavement.

22

'Love Removal Machine' – The Cult

I didn't see the boat until we landed in it. It was sitting low in the canal on the far side of the concrete embankment, hidden among a row of blue tarped gondolas and a narrow water taxi with a glass canopy and a battered hull. My right foot plunged forward, my ankle twisting as the rest of my weight came down on it, and I slammed face-first into one of the seats.

Blackness . . .

Wait.

I grabbed the moment and dragged myself back up into consciousness through sheer willpower. Momentum took hold of me and I rolled backwards across the deck, trying to hold on to something that wasn't actively attempting to pull away from me. The blow to the face had made my eyes water, honing my senses to stinging awareness, and I smelled open seawater and the coppery odor of my own blood trickling from my nostrils. The boat's motor was deafening. Up at the wheel, Gobi swerved through the canal. I sat up and saw the lights of the bridge coming up. It was too low for us to pass under it.

'I told you I had other targets in Venice.'

'Armitage?' I shouted.

Gobi jammed the throttle all the way forward so the bow of the boat spiked higher in the air, as if she could somehow intimidate the bridge into getting out of our way. For a second I thought about jumping out, but we were going too fast and I'd heard about people getting sucked back into the motor, which at this point might have been a blessing. I looked straight ahead, less than twenty meters from impact. At this distance, there was no question. We were either going to crash straight into the stone buttresses or decapitate ourselves – it just wasn't high enough.

'Gobi!' I shouted, one last attempt. 'Don't!'

Then it was too late and we were underneath it, the

cavernous low-hanging darkness lunging forward. I ducked, dropping down to my hands and knees, and heard the bridge rip off the top of the glass canopy, covering my shoulders and head in a brittle spray of glass, splintering metal and wood. There was a scraping screech and the boat stopped, stuck halfway underneath arching stone.

I breathed. It was dark under here, cold, the only light coming from the glow of the instrument panel. Up front, Gobi was still leaning forward, draped over the wheel.

Sirens.

I got ready to jump.

'Wait.'

I looked around. In the shadows off to our right, I saw a second boat floating just a foot or two away, tied to a ringbolt under the bridge. It had been sitting here the whole time.

Reaching over, Gobi pulled the knots, leaned in, and started the engine. She flicked a switch and I saw a red light blinking under the console of the other boat. Still leaning over, she nudged the throttle forward and sent it out the far side of the canal. As it disappeared I realized it looked like ours, the one we were in now.

I looked at her. The first wave of adrenaline had passed

141

and left me feeling wrung out and shaky, full of questions that needed immediate answers.

'Why did you do it?' My voice was shaking so hard that I could barely get the words out. 'Why did you kill Armitage? He didn't – '

From out on the far side of the bridge, an explosion tore a hole through the world. It wasn't so much loud as simply big – *BIG* – and it shook the entire canal, pulsed through the water around us, bouncing off the sides of ancient buildings so hard that I actually thought I saw them tremble. My mind flashed to the second boat that had been waiting here, the one that looked like ours, the one she'd sent out, the decoy. A moment later, I smelled smoke pouring up the canal, thick and acrid.

Gobi never took her eyes off me. I felt a jagged lump in my throat, filling my sinuses, pushing up into the bottoms of my eyes. There was only one question left, and I didn't want to ask it. Not that it mattered.

'What about Paula?'

Gobi didn't say anything.

'What about Paula?'

'She would have killed you.'

'Why?'

A slight shrug. 'You had served your purpose.'

'What was that, exactly?'

'Drawing me into the open, so Armitage's hired guns could take me down.'

I thought of the gunfire from above. 'That sniper on the rooftop . . . ?'

'There was more than one. Armitage meant to turn the plaza into a killing box.'

'A killing box,' I said. 'That's great. A freaking *killing* box? Why?'

'Because he knew that I was coming for him.'

I glared at her and felt angry tears pricking in my eyes that had nothing to do with the smoke. They were rising up from the pit where my stomach had once been, a space that was now somehow hollow and sickly heavy at the same time, a deep aching place, like someone had kicked my heart in the balls.

'How long have you been . . . hunting him?'

'Kaya gave me assignment four months ago, after New York. But Armitage knew.'

I thought about the gunshots that had come from the

rooftops overhead, snipers on the cathedral.

'Armitage knew it was you coming for him?'

Gobi nodded.

'For how long?'

'At least since August, he has been trying to draw me out.'

August. The sickness inside me folded over on top of itself like a map of conquered territory, and for a moment I was miserably sure I was going to throw up. My mind flashed to the night I'd met Paula at the party in Brooklyn, how fortuitous the whole thing had been, the way she had initiated our first conversation and everything afterward. How incredulous I'd been that such a hot woman would be interested in me. Drawing me in. Then the invitation to Europe. Then Venice. Then the gun.

Move and he dies.

'You were only a pawn, Perry,' Gobi said. 'How do you say, *leverage* . . . for them to find me.'

My throat felt tight. I didn't say anything.

'Is time to go.'

'No.' I took a step back and my heel bumped into something black piled under the seat in front of me. Diving suits and masks. Oxygen tanks. Regulators.

'Oh, no,' I said. 'No way.'

Gobi was moving faster now, putting on the wetsuit.

'Screw that. I'm not doing this. I'm *done.*'

She spat in the mask and rinsed it with water from the canal, checked the oxygen gauge, and looked up at me. The sirens were very close now.

'It's an island,' I said. 'They'll just keep looking for you.'

'Not now.' She nodded in the direction of the explosion. 'We are dead. At least until they do not recover bodies.'

'We can't just – '

Gobi thrust a pair of swim fins toward me.

'I'm not going any farther,' I said. 'I'm calling my dad, he'll get a lawyer. I'm going home.'

'That is not possible anymore.'

'Why not?'

She looked up at me one more time through the swim mask, staring right through me. I saw something new in her face then. Sadness.

That was when she held up Paula's iPad.

23

'If There's a Rocket Tie Me to It' – Snow Patrol

The screen had cracked back at the café, but it still worked.

I stared at it and felt the world go sideways.

In the picture on the screen, my mom and dad and Annie were sitting on a wooden bench in a room with no windows. The walls behind them were dirty white, the color of March snow. It was a very clear image. The resolution was excellent. Dad was holding a copy of the *New York Times* up to the camera so I could see today's date. His chin was already starting to show the beginnings of stubble. Mom's eyes were bloodshot, the tip of her nose red, like she'd been crying. But Annie was the worst. She was wearing a dirty pink T-shirt and her favorite pair of jeans, hugging herself, and her face just looked blank, like inside her head she'd gone to find a place where she wouldn't have to be scared anymore.

'Where are they?' I heard myself ask.

Gobi shook her head. 'I do not know.'

'What?'

'Is Paula's iPad,' Gobi said. 'If I had not come tonight, she would have used this picture on you.'

'For what?'

'To get to me.'

I shook my head. 'No.'

'Leverage, Perry. Think.'

The sirens were practically on top of us now.

I looked at the iPad again.

'Armitage did this?'

Gobi nodded.

'And you killed him.'

'It was assignment,' Gobi said.

'Screw your assignment! Your assignment got my family kidnapped!' I wanted to throw the iPad at her as hard as I could. 'You shot Armitage! The cops wouldn't even know where to start looking for them!'

'Is not a police matter.'

'What?'

She just looked at me. 'I must finish.'

'What are you talking about?'

'Kaya gave me multiple targets. Monash was first, then Armitage.' She glanced away. 'There is one more.'

'Who?'

'You know.'

Of course I did. 'Paula.'

'She was right about the shotgun being empty. But we were out of time. If I had paused to reload, and finish her off, the other snipers would have killed me.'

'Hold on.' I was trying not to lose any remaining control I might still have over my sympathetic nervous system, which didn't seem to be feeling very sympathetic toward me right now. 'If she's the only one left who knows where my family is, then we need her alive.'

Gobi held up Paula's iPad, then slipped it into a watertight packet and sealed it shut. 'We have everything we need.'

'Are you sure?'

'Not until we get a chance to look at it closely.' She

looked around. 'We need to get out of here.'

She didn't have to ask again. I had already started putting on the wetsuit.

24

'Hold Your Colour' – Pendulum

Two people pulled out of Venice that night on a Eurostar sleeper, a man and a woman who didn't give the city so much as a backwards glance. They were traveling under the names Myra Abrams and John Galt, carrying full sets of ID retrieved from a train station locker, along with clean sets of clothes.

Before we left, there had been a whispered conversation on the platform, neither of us looking at the other:

'How do you know they won't follow us?'

'They will.'

'What?'

'The second boat will not stall them forever.'

'Then what?'

She had brought out a folder bulging with receipts and itineraries. 'I have booked three different flights out of Venice Airport. Four sets of train tickets. Two rental cars. All of this will buy us time.'

But how much time, Gobi?

How much is enough?

•   . • ·•

After the conductor came by for our passports, the compartment lights were dimmed and she retrieved the iPad from the waterproof bag where she'd stowed it. She'd changed into a white T-shirt and a leather jacket and jeans, her hair tucked back under a green Mao cap with a low brim that did a decent job of covering her face. At first glance she looked like any other young traveler whiling away the long night. Glancing over her shoulder, I flicked my gaze over the first CNN headlines trumpeting the assassination of George Armitage without really seeing them. It had taken less than an hour for the shock wave to go global. Gobi didn't offer the iPad, and I didn't ask to see it. Anything of Paula's that I had to touch, I wanted to bleach first. It felt as contaminated as my memories of her.

Instead, I looked down at the folder of rail receipts and unused tickets.

'So where are we really going?'

'Zermatt.'

'Why?'

She held up the iPad. 'There is someone who might help us with this. Tracking the picture. Finding your family.'

'Well, try not to kill them before they do.'

'If it is not too late.'

'Why would it be too late?'

Gobi looked like she might not answer the question, but then at the last moment she relented. 'Armitage was only holding your family to get to me. Now he is dead. Is only a matter of time.'

'Before what? You mean before the rest of his organization decides not to keep them alive anymore?'

This time she really didn't say anything.

'How much time?'

Again, no answer. Not that I really expected one at this point. 'Maybe the cops – ' I started.

'Perry, I told you.' Her hand found my wrist and held it. 'No police in the world can help you with this now.'

'You don't know that.'

'You want to get off this train?' She pointed out at the dark Italian countryside speeding by. 'Next stop, take your chances? Be my guest. Tell your story to authorities. See how far it gets you.'

'Maybe I will.'

We held our positions like that for a few seconds, neither of us saying anything. Then, hating her more than ever, I pointed at the image of Armitage on the screen.

'Who was he really?'

'A target.'

'What else?'

'That is all.'

'So why did this Kaya guy hire you to – '

She let out a shuddery breath that didn't sound much like her at all. 'I am tired, Perry.'

'Yeah, well, I'm really sorry about that, but if it weren't for you killing these people, my family and I wouldn't be in this situation, so I think I'm entitled to some kind of explanation, don't you?'

She reached up and switched off the overhead light. We sat in the darkness for a long moment, rocking back and forth with the motion of the train, and finally she spoke again.

'In a past life,' Gobi said, 'Armitage helped people buy things.'

'What kind of things?'

'Weapons.' Gobi gestured with her hand, a so-so gesture. 'He was, how do you say, *tarpininkas* . . . a go-between?'

'So why did your guy Kaya want him dead?'

'Bad blood.'

'They were related?'

'Former partners. They dealt with the same fringe groups. Third world dictators. African warlords. Providing them with the weapons they needed. When Armitage went legitimate ten years ago, Kaya began to worry about his old partner's discretion.'

'So Kaya hired you to kill Armitage, Monash, and Paula?'

'Not hired,' Gobi said.

'Why do you keep saying that?' I was trying to keep my voice down in the sleeping train compartment, but it wasn't easy. 'If they're not paying you to kill all these people, then why are you doing it?'

She didn't answer, not even when I finally got tired of waiting, reached for her arm, and pulled her toward me. Her head lolled sideways, and in the light of a passing railway trestle, I saw the whites of her eyes rolled back in her head. A seizure, at the worst possible moment. She never seemed to have them at any other time.

'Gobi?' Her skin felt cold, clammy, and when I tried to shake her, her limbs were loose, without any resistance in the muscles or the joints.

I touched her face and felt something sticky and wet.

At first I thought maybe it was sweat. Then I looked at my fingers and saw they were red. Blood was trickling from her nose and the corner of her lips, covering her chin and neck. She had already soaked the whole front of her T-shirt.

'Oh, shit,' I said, lifting her limp body. 'Gobi . . . What the hell?'

Her mouth fell open and she made a clicking noise. There was still a lot of blood coming from her nose, and maybe her mouth too. Out of nowhere I thought about what the guy with the beard, Swierczynski, had said to us last night.

The bullet is already in your head.

I tried to think clearly about what was happening. The blood didn't make sense. She hadn't been shot back in St. Mark's Square, and there was no way she was really walking around with an actual bullet in her head.

I picked up her wrist and felt her pulse. It was irregular, and when I watched her chest rise, her breathing seemed shallow and labored.

'Look, I don't know what to do here,' I said. 'Is there an injection or something I can give you?'

Her eyes flicked toward me silent and helpless. When she still didn't say anything, I reached down and started digging through the canvas tote she'd dragged from the locker back at the Venice train station. Inside were our fake passports and documents, two bottles of water, a silk scarf, sunglasses, a Eurail map and train schedule, a thick bundle of euros, a tube of lipstick, and a few bullets rolling around. No medicine, no messages, no clues.

At the very bottom, my hand came across a key tucked into one of the seams. It was a big chunk of brass, and at first I thought it was the room key from Venice. Then I realized there was a different tag on it completely. It read, in total:

Hotel Schoeneweiss, Zermatt

I dropped the key back in her bag, poured some water on the scarf, and tried to wipe some of the blood from her face, zipping up her jacket to cover the stained shirt. I guess I knew where we were heading after all.

Next to me, Gobi had started to tremble.

25

'Everybody Daylight' – Brightblack Morning Light

I awoke without realizing that I'd fallen asleep. The train was slowing down, the rhythm of its wheels changing, sloughing off speed, drawing me from sleep so deep, it felt like waking up from anesthesia or hypnosis. I'd been hypnotized once at a party, and coming out of it had felt like this, blurry and unpleasant. *I'm going to begin counting back from ten, and when I get to one you'll be fully awake . . .*

I sat up. My mouth was dry, and getting my eyes completely open was probably going to require a couple of toothpicks and a whole lot of caffeine.

We were pulling into the station. The video screen at the front of the car said we were in Zermatt. I glanced around, immediately on guard for anybody who might have been watching us, but the only other passengers on this side of the compartment were a pair of hippie backpackers, a guy and a girl slouched side by side under a heavy Hudson Bay blanket, their sleeping bodies shifting together, keeping time with the train's still diminishing velocity.

Next to me, Gobi slumped pale and motionless against my shoulder. Sometime during the night she had finally stopped trembling and slipped into a kind of shallow doze. I had a foggy memory of changing trains, getting off the TGV in the middle of the night, helping her through some desolate border checkpoint at three a.m., past two midnight-shift porters leering at us from behind a closed magazine kiosk, muttering something in broken, learned-from-TV English about a boy bringing his whore home after a rough night. From there we'd boarded a Swiss regional, handing our passports and tickets to a listless-looking official, who'd stamped them and shoved them back.

Now we'd come to a complete stop, the first rays of sun spiking down from the Alps, filling the compartment with brittle orange light that I wasn't remotely prepared for.

'Wake up.'

'Ugh?'

'We're here.' I moved my arm, and Gobi stirred reluctantly toward consciousness, making a gravelly noise in her throat. Standing up, I lifted under her arm, pulling her down the aisle and guiding her down the steps to the main platform until she started to support her own weight. Outside the air was sharp and glacial and smelled faintly like pine trees – an almost painfully clean smell. I slipped the sunglasses over Gobi's eyes to cover as much of her face as possible, and hauled her out into the daylight.

The terminal clock said it was just past seven a.m. Outside the station, the first early skiers and tourists were already on their way to the slopes. The main drag had no actual cars, just these little diesel vehicles and electric mini-taxis shuttling people past chalets and still closed alpine shops full of overpriced watches, postcards, and cuckoo clocks. A decorative red and green banner blowing in the wind over the street advertised some kind of festival:

ClauWau Fest!! - 25-27 Nov

I handed one of the drivers a twenty-euro bill from Gobi's

bag and asked him to drive us to the Hotel Schoeneweiss.

'Wohin?' He gazed at me blankly, a grizzled middle-aged man in a golf cap with windburned hangdog jowls, watery gray eyes, and a gunslinger's mustache hanging off his upper lip.

'Is there a problem?' I asked, trying to support Gobi's head without making it look like that's what I was doing.

'There is no such hotel in Zermatt, *mein Herr.*'

'There has to be.' I held up the key that I'd found in Gobi's bag so he could read the label. 'Look.'

The driver inspected the key for a long moment and gestured gloomily for us to climb in.

• • • •

At the far end of the main street, past all the other inns and shops, the taxi pulled up in front of a small wooden storefront that seemed to be built directly into the side of the mountain itself. The shop window was full of dusty wine bottles. The hand-carved sign above the low arched door read VINOTHEKE — WEINE — SPIRITUOSEN.

'Looks like a liquor store,' I said. With its low, cavelike

entrance and folksy décor, it looked like where Bilbo Baggins might drop by for a bottle of *eiswein*. 'Are you sure this is it?'

The driver grunted and pointed above it, to an even smaller row of windows above the wine and spirits shop. A tiny hand-carved shingle no bigger than a license plate was creaking back and forth in the breeze: SCHOENEWEISS.

I looked at the darkened front door. 'Where do we check in?'

'The Hotel Schoeneweiss never has any guests.'

'Sounds like a great place,' I muttered, and when I opened the back door to help Gobi out of the cab, she slouched over sideways and tumbled forward into my arms. I barely managed to catch her, and when I did, I saw how much worse she'd gotten.

Her half-lidded eyes were glazed and glassy, like she'd forgotten how to blink. Her cracked lips hung slightly parted, and at that point I honestly couldn't tell if she was breathing or not. Her nose and mouth had started to bleed again, not much, but enough to drizzle down over her chin. I knelt down over her and glanced back up at the driver.

'Is there a hospital around here?'

The driver took one glance at Gobi, decided that he'd done his part for the cause, and hit the gas and sped off, leaving us there at the end of the street. The enormity of my bad decision-making – my misplaced trust in others and myself – settled over me like one of those smallpox-infected blankets that the U.S. Cavalry supposedly handed out to the Plains Indians. Why hadn't I just taken my chances with the Italian police?

Some bleak inner-Perry gave voice to my darkest suspicions: *Because they would have arrested you, and she would have died, and your family would never have been found.*

The cold reality of it shot through me, a steel instrument tapping a raw nerve. Every second that I hesitated, every moment that I let slip away, meant that my dad and mom and Annie were getting that much closer to –

To death. You know it. That's exactly the word.

I was trying to decide if I should just start looking around for some kind of emergency clinic somewhere when a cold hand gripped the back of my neck, thumb and forefingers pinching the tendons there, and a sharp bolt of pain shot down both arms just before they went completely numb.

The German voice in my ear was calm, almost a whisper.

'Let me see her.'

26

'Hurt' – Nine Inch Nails

'Let me guess,' I said. 'Kaya?'

The man standing behind me didn't answer. I put him mid-to-late-thirties, handsome in a sloppy kind of way. He was wearing brown wool pants with a faded flannel shirt, sleeves rolled up to his forearms, with two-day stubble and thick black hair that tumbled across his forehead. He had quick, searching eyes and the kind of sharp upper lip and chin that could have made him a late-night movie star from the fifties, except right now he didn't seem to give much of a shit what he looked like at all.

'Help me get her inside,' he said, in that same low

German voice. And then, touching Gobi's chin gently, turning her head: 'It is all right now, Zusane. I'm here.'

· ·•·•

We carried her inside the empty wine store, a cramped rectangle of darkness that looked as if nobody had bought champagne or anything else here in years. As we walked past the front counter with its hooded cash register, I noticed that each shelf held exactly one row of bottles, enough to give the outward appearance of a well-stocked market. Not only were most of the bottles empty, but they were covered in about an inch of dust.

In the back, the shop gave way to a set of double doors that opened onto a narrow stairwell. I was holding Gobi's legs and the guy took her arms, backing his way carefully up the steps while I did my best to keep her feet from dragging.

'How long has she been like this?' he asked.

'Since last night.' I looked up at him. 'Who – '

'Through here.' At the top of the stairs we stepped through a doorway into a blinding expanse of light. In contrast to the gloomy booze shop below, the second floor was a spotless pine-floored room with a back wall that was one gigantic mirror.

It took me a second to realize that it was a gym.

We carried Gobi past weights and barbells, an arrangement of parallel bars, beams, tumbling mats, even a pommel horse, with a floor-to-ceiling climbing wall occupying the wall behind it. Boxing gear – heavy bags, throwing dummies, speed bags – dangled from the ceiling. The far end was dedicated to all kinds of increasingly dangerous-looking martial arts stuff, sparring gloves and masks and projectile weapons, swords, knives, and an enormous padlocked gun rack gleaming with enough well-oiled automatic firepower to blow this corner of Switzerland off the map. The cumulative effect was like taking an evolutionary speed-tour of the ultimate adolescent revenge fantasy, from 'first I'll get strong' to 'then they'll be sorry.' Taken in all at once, it was more than a little disturbing.

'Where do you keep the nuke?' I asked.

Ignoring me, the man opened a door on the opposite side of the gym. Inside, I glimpsed residential decor – marble floors, a long leather sofa, steel and glass end tables, recessed light fixtures. I thought I heard a Hawaiian steel guitar playing somewhere softly inside.

'Stay here.'

'Now hold on – '

He took Gobi inside and shut the door in my face.

27

'99 Problems' – Jay-Z

Which was very uncool.

I wandered restlessly around the gym, checking out all the black iron and chrome and not really seeing any of it, thinking of all the things that had gone wrong so far and waiting for the guy to come back out. When he didn't, I went back to the other door leading back downstairs, but the handle wouldn't budge. Apparently on top of everything else, I was now locked inside the biggest, most lethal workout room in the universe.

My empty stomach swung open its vaults with a growl that wasn't so much hunger as an overall complaint about conditions in general. Sometime in the middle of the night

I'd gnawed on some strangely shaped Bavarian chocolate cookie that came in a purple plastic egg, and chased it down with two cans of some sticky-sweet German energy drink, but when was the last time I'd eaten real food?

What about your parents and Annie? You think anyone's giving them anything?

My thoughts circled back to the three of them, locked up wherever they were, and I felt a little ashamed for thinking of myself and my problems. I hoped they were at least giving them bathroom breaks. Annie in particular used to get weird whenever she had to hold it, like on long trips in the car.

Thinking about that, the three of them but Annie especially, I felt a piercing blade of anger at Armitage and what he'd done. What kind of scumbag does something like that to a little girl? For twenty-four hours, I'd equated George Armitage with a record deal and rock superstardom. Now all that was gone forever – it had never really existed in the first place – and I was glad he was dead.

Unless his being dead was going to cost my family their lives.

Don't think about it, a voice inside my head suggested.

Except, that technique hadn't been working any better

lately then it ever had. Instead, I found myself gazing at the locked rack of machine guns, pistols, and rifles, row upon row of them gleaming like the black grin of war itself.

That was when the door opened and the guy came back out.

‘Perhaps we should start with introductions.’ He was wiping his hands off with a towel, flexing his fingers, making big, muscular-looking fists, the kind that seemed to come with double the normal number of knuckles and veins. ‘I know who you are, but you do not know me. My name is not Kaya. I do not know who this Kaya is.’

‘No offense,’ I said, ‘but I really don’t care much about the whole meet and greet right now. The only reason I’m even here with Gobi now is that she thought maybe we could find –’

‘Your family,’ the man said, ‘yes. You are referring to Phillip and Julie Stormaire and your twelve-year-old sister, Annie, last known residence, one-fifteen Cedar Terrace, East Norwalk, Connecticut, whereabouts currently unknown.’

173

'How did you know that?'

'She told me.'

'Gobi?'

'Zusane.'

I nodded. Zusane had been Gobi's given name before she'd taken on the name of her dead sister, Gobija, and smuggled herself into New York to take revenge on a soulless human cancer named Santamaria. It all felt like so long ago that it could have happened to a completely different guy.

'I am Erich Schoeneweiss.' He reached into his pocket and took out the key that I'd found in Gobi's bag, then began turning it over in his hand. 'You should know that bringing Zusane here was the most dangerous thing you could have done.' He glanced up at me. 'You probably also saved her life.'

'You can thank me later.'

'I am making inquiries now as to the whereabouts of your family. They may yield something useful, or they may not. We will know soon.'

'How soon?'

'An hour, perhaps two.'

'And then what?'

'That is your decision,' he said, and I noticed for the first time how colorless his eyes were, an almost silvery gray-white, like the ice that hardens on top of old snow, the kind that can cut your ankle if you step through it the wrong way. 'All I ask is that if you do choose to notify the authorities, please use discretion regarding my own involvement.'

'Don't mention your name,' I nodded. 'I get it.' I looked at him. 'Why did you say that bringing Gobi here is the most dangerous thing I could have done?'

Erich hesitated as if weighing his words carefully. Before he could formulate an answer, the door behind us swung open and Gobi stepped out.

Right away I couldn't believe how much better she looked. She was wearing a plain white flannel nightgown and slippers, with her hair wrapped up in a towel. The color had returned to her cheeks, and her eyes looked clear and bright, totally alert and oriented to her surroundings.

After walking over to Erich, she leaned in, took his hand, and murmured something to him in German. He smiled and answered back, squeezing her fingers. Then she looked to me.

'Thank you, Perry.'

'Sure,' I said stiffly. 'I mean, you know, whatever. I found the key in your bag, and I didn't know what else to do, so . . .'

'You did the right thing.' Gobi looked across the gymnasium and stretched up on her toes. 'I spent three years in this room,' she said, 'getting ready for my trip to United States.'

'You trained here?' I turned to Erich. 'With him?'

She glanced up at him, and Erich nodded with that same cool, expressionless look in his eyes. 'In this country,' he said, 'every male must serve in the armed forces. After my father got out, he started this . . . hotel. We operated it together until his death, and I took over by myself. It is not really a hotel.'

'Gee, really?' I eyed the rows of machine guns mounted on the walls. 'I was just going to ask about the minibar.'

Erich smiled politely. 'There is a saying in certain intelligence community circles. "Herr Schoeneweiss runs a hotel in Zermatt that never has any guests." However, we do offer accommodations to special clients on a private basis.'

'Special clients?'

'Not everything that I teach here is strictly legal. In

fact, some of it is very illegal. There is a soundproof firing and demolition range in the basement. Intelligence, survival, evasion and interrogation tactics, wiretapping and surveillance. The only thing I do not give instruction on is – '

'Driving?'

Erich raised one eyebrow, surprised for the first time. 'How did you know?'

'Lucky guess.' I was thinking of Broadway, down by Union Square, the smoking-rubber smell of the Jaguar's tires as I'd made the turn onto Fourteenth Street with Gobi next to me, calculating distances. 'I've done a bit of that myself.'

●. . ●. ●

Erich finally let me back into his living quarters, where I caught a shower and changed into an anonymous pair of slightly too-big jeans and a black long-sleeved T-shirt that nonetheless felt great compared to the uber-stylish Euro-suit I'd been wearing since Venice. When I came out, he was in the kitchen, dicing garlic while Gobi made a fruit salad. I stood there while she speed-chopped pineapple, mango, and cantaloupe. It was like watching some high-octane mashup of black ops and the Food Network.

'What's that?' I asked.

'Spinach frittata.'

'Not that.' I pointed. *That.*

Erich glanced over his shoulder into the adjacent room, at the computer monitor on the desk. I recognized Paula's iPad, wired into the CPU as an endless row of IP addresses scrolled upward across the screen.

'I am scanning the incoming and outgoing messages through the iPad, specifically the e-mail of the photo she received. Depending on the level of encryption that your girlfriend was using – '

'Ex-girlfriend.'

'Of course.'

I took a breath. 'Any luck?'

'Some, yes.' He walked over to the desk and clicked the mouse, slowing the data flow to check individual lines of code. 'Unfortunately, it looks as though Armitage's people are rerouting messages through several other servers. According to this, your family may be in Reykjavik, Port-au-Prince, or Las Vegas, or any of several European cities.'

'You can't pinpoint it any better than that?'

'It will take more time. And perhaps faster equipment than I have here.' He produced a cell phone and glanced down at Gobi as he stepped out of the room. 'Excuse me.'

I waited until the door clicked shut behind him, and looked across the table at Gobi. She had finished with the salad and was looking around for something else to chop up.

'So, when you were training with him, did you, you know . . . stay here?'

She smiled a little and put down the knife. 'You mean, did we sleep together?'

'Forget it,' I said. 'Not my business.'

'When I first came here, my life had been torn apart by what happened to my sister.' The smile slipped away. 'I was consumed by rage and grief. Erich taught me many things.'

'Okay.'

She raised an eyebrow. 'You should not ask questions, Perry, if you do not want answers.'

'Whatever.'

'You are jealous.'

'Please.' I felt the tips of my ears glowing hot, a feeling that I hated, especially because I knew it was obvious to anyone looking at me that I was blushing. 'You and me – '

'Are you still virgin, yes?'

'Okay,' I said, '*so* not a relevant topic of conversation at this point.'

'That woman Paula. All the time that you were together, you and she did not ever – '

'She wasn't the one,' I blurted out. I don't know where *that* came from. I certainly didn't intend on telling Gobi any more than I already had about my own life, and up till that moment, I'd never really thought about why Paula and I hadn't had sex. I'd just assumed it was my hang-up, virginal inertia, fear of the unknown, whatever it was, and dealt with it in private, on my own. Yet here we were in the middle of Switzerland, dissecting the whole thing under bright lights like the squirming toad that it was.

'You are looking for the quiet type?' she asked.

'Actually,' I said, 'at this point I'd settle for the not-actively-trying-to-kill-me type.'

'I read all those e-mails you sent, Perry. Every last one.' Now she was sitting directly in front of me, so close that I could hear her breathing. 'You know how hard it was for me not to answer? To not tell you where I was?'

'Yeah, well, you did the right thing,' I said. 'I mean, we can't even share the same continent without somebody turning up dead.'

She made a mock frown. 'Is deal-breaker then?'

'What?'

'Me and you.'

'Is bigtime deal-breaker, yeah.'

'Well, whoever she is' – Gobi smiled again and picked up the dishes, putting them in the sink – 'I hope you find her before you get yourself killed.'

28

'King of Pain' – The Police

After a late breakfast I lay down on Erich's couch, propped my head on the armrest, and let my eyelids sink shut. I'd only intended to rest for a minute, but last night's trip must have completely sandbagged me, because when I finally opened my eyes, long shadows had filled the studio, and it felt like evening.

'What time is it?' I sat up, disoriented, trying to make sense of the room around me. 'How long have I been asleep?'

Erich looked down at me. 'Most of the day.'

'You didn't wake me up?'

'You looked like you could use the rest.' He was wearing a white *judogi* with a thick belt and heavy weave that I only recognized because I'd taken a year of judo back when I was nine.

'What's going on? What did I miss?'

'Erich?' Gobi's voice came from the doorway. She was looking at Erich's white martial arts uniform, an expression of pure, childlike pleasure on her face. 'Can we?'

'You must promise,' Erich said. 'Not full strength.'

Gobi nodded. 'I will show mercy on you.'

'I meant for your sake.'

'I know what you meant,' she said, and followed him into the gym.

• •▪ •▪

Twenty minutes later, after Gobi had grabbed Erich and flipped him over her shoulder onto a pile of gym mats, I watched him walk over to where I was standing – okay, cowering – in the corner by the gun rack. He was sweating and breathing hard, rubbing his elbow and grinning ruefully.

'I'd hate to see full strength,' I said.

He didn't answer right away. On the other side of the

gym, Gobi stood barefoot, emptying a bottle of water over her head, shaking the droplets off her hair. She was wearing a matching *judogi* to Erich's, and it fit her curves perfectly, as if it had been custom-made and waiting here for her to come back.

In the sparring ring, she and Erich had moved together like two people who knew each other's bodies on an intimate level, striking and spinning and taking hold of each other with a level of familiarity, even pleasure, that told me everything I could've already guessed about their former relationship. Watching them had made me feel like a voyeur, as if I were spying on something private.

After they'd finished, I looked around at the other bags and sparring gear, then back at Erich, and said the words I thought I'd never speak.

'Teach me to fight.'

Erich looked at me out of the corner of his eye, bemused. 'I do not think so.'

'I *do* think so.' I stood up. 'Come on, right now, let's go.'

'Perry, I spent three years training Zusane.'

'Her name's Gobi,' I said.

'Regardless. The conditioning alone takes a lifetime of discipline.'

'Oh yeah?' Already the logical side of my brain realized that of course he was right. What I wanted was the equivalent of that scene in *The Matrix* where Neo needs to be able to fly a helicopter and just plugs the information instantaneously into his brain. 'We'll just see about that.'

'Why do you suddenly want to learn how to fight?'

'Self-defense.'

'Against . . . ?'

'You know, whoever.'

Erich looked at me thoughtfully. The clear, nearly colorless disks of his eyes seemed to take my full measure, and as much as it irritated me, I felt like what he was seeing was probably an accurate indication of who I was at that moment – desperate, way out of my league, the emotional equivalent of a naked mole rat.

'You do not need to worry about her.'

'Oh, really?' I asked, wondering if he had any idea of what she'd put me through so far.

Erich just shook his head. 'She will always have your back. Simply say to her, *As tave myliu.*'

'What's that mean?'

He smiled again, faintly. 'Just some conversational Lithuanian.'

'Perry?' Gobi had ambled over, her hair and uniform soaked and, I couldn't help but notice, semi-transparent, clinging to her skin with the water she'd dumped over it. She offered me her hand. 'Do you want to play?'

· ·•·•

We started with judo. It was also where we ended. Gobi said she'd show me a basic two-armed shoulder throw, as simple as it got. Then she stuck her elbow under my arm and before I knew it I was upside down on the floor, my spine feeling like it was shattered like a discarded jigsaw puzzle.

'Perry?' Her face and Erich's appeared above me, looking down, neither of them looking especially concerned. 'You are okay?'

I tried to say no. But talking involved breathing, and I still hadn't figured out how to do that. After a moment I heard Gobi say something about hitting the shower, and

I discovered that, left alone, I could probably crawl back to my feet.

• · •·—●

'She is not well,' Erich said as the two of us walked back into the living quarters.

'Her?' I managed, trying to ignore the cracked-open feeling across my sternum, as if someone had done open-heart surgery on me without putting me to sleep first. 'What about me?'

'She told me that she failed to complete her mission in Venice.'

'Armitage? Believe me, she didn't fail.'

'The *first* target,' Erich said. 'The man disguised as a priest. It was the first time that ever happened.'

'Yeah, I guess.' I thought of the bald guy in the steamer trunk opening his eyes in the canal, and looked back at Gobi in the gym. 'But she seems okay now.'

'The corticosteroids that I gave her stopped the bleeding and restored her strength temporarily, but . . .' Erich shook his head. 'I am not a doctor. My medical skills are limited to emergency field trauma techniques that I learned in the Swiss army, and also what I have picked up over the years here. But since I saw her last, her condition has worsened considerably.'

'You mean the epilepsy?'

He stared at me. 'Is that what she told you? That she had epilepsy?'

'Yeah. Temporal lobe epilepsy. Like Van Gogh. Why?'

Erich didn't say anything.

'You're saying she doesn't?'

'Epilepsy does not normally cause internal bleeding. Or such intense and prolonged states of dementia.'

'When was she having dementia?'

'When you first brought her here,' he said, 'she was very disoriented. She told me that you were her final target. She swore she'd been hired to kill you.'

'*What?*'

Erich shook his head. 'If you ask her now, she claims not to remember. But at the time . . .'

'So if it's not epilepsy,' I said, 'what's making her act like this?'

'Did she ever tell you how she got that scar on her throat?'

'No,' I said, following after him. 'Why?'

Erich walked through the living room to where the computers were still hooked up to Paula's iPad and began typing, not looking at me.

'Wait a second, what happened?'

'What happened to who?' Gobi asked behind me. I looked around and saw that she was still dressed in her *judogi,* sipping a tall glass of water. Her gaze flashed from me to Erich, and back to me again. When neither of us answered her, she set the glass down and took another step toward us, repeating the same question with quiet intensity. 'What are you talking about?'

Then the typing sounds continued and I heard a voice coming from across the room, from the computer monitors hooked up to Paula's iPad.

It was my father's voice.

29

'Family Man' – Hall & Oates

'I don't know where she went,' Dad was saying through the speakers. 'I don't know when she's coming back.'

I peered over Erich's shoulder at the monitor. On the screen, Mom, Dad, and Annie were still sitting on the floor of the same dirty white room they'd been photographed in earlier, none of them looking at the camera. Annie was asleep, and Mom was holding her head and shoulders in her arms, cradling her like a baby. If you didn't know any better, you might have guessed they were three stranded travelers in the United terminal at O'Hare, waiting for the weather to clear. Dad had rolled his shirt sleeves up. The newspaper that he had been holding earlier lay in a rumpled gray pile next to him, along with some empty plates and wrappers and Evian bottles. That made me feel a little better. At least someone was giving them food and water.

Mom glanced at Dad. 'Are you going to try to talk to her?' she asked, in a low voice, as if she didn't want to disturb Annie, but the microphone picked it up clearly.

'I don't know what you expect me to say,' Dad said.

'You certainly didn't seem to have any problems with that earlier.'

He looked at my mom. 'Really, Julie? We're really going to get into this now?'

'I should have known,' Mom said tonelessly, staring at the floor, rubbing her temples, a gesture that I associated with a very specific moment in their marriage, two years ago. 'I should. Have. Known.'

'Oh, like you've been a saint yourself lately,' Dad said, loud enough that Annie stirred on my mom's lap.

'Keep your voice down. What's wrong with you?'

Dad didn't say anything, and that only seemed to make Mom madder.

'Don't you dare try to make this about me,' she said. 'This has nothing to do with that.'

My dad reached up and ran his hands through what was left of his hair. 'Julie, we're locked in a room with no idea who's doing this or when they're coming back. I don't particularly give a shit what old boyfriend you're flirting with on Facebook.'

'Wait.' I looked at Erich. 'Is this live?'

'No,' Erich said. 'It is a QuickTime file. An attachment. It came through the iPad just a few minutes ago.'

'Can you get any idea of where it came from?'

'There is more.' Erich clicked on the PLAY triangle again.

I immediately wished that he hadn't.

'Your son's girlfriend,' Mom was saying. 'Tell me, Phil, just out of curiosity, is there a depth to which you wouldn't sink?'

Dad took in a breath and let it out. Maybe it was the angle, but he didn't look like himself at all anymore. 'I already told you, nothing happened.'

'And I'm supposed to believe that?'

'Right now, honestly, I don't care what you believe.'

It was the wrong thing to say on every possible level, and I wanted to reach through the screen and strangle him for it. Meanwhile, Mom's whole body sort of folded in on itself and she just started crying. It was a terrible sound, hoarse and scratchy, like she was coming down with a cold. In her sleep, Annie shifted a little on her lap, drew her knees up, and tucked in her arms but didn't wake up. I just hoped she was really asleep.

'Look,' Dad said, 'that's not what I meant.' When he reached over to try to put his arm on my mother's shoulder, she jerked away.

'Don't touch me.'

'Julie – '

'Don't.'

'Okay,' he said, sounding tired. 'But I want you to listen to me. I don't know why this is happening. I don't know what we're doing here. Obviously Paula isn't who she said she was.'

'Obviously.' The bitterness dripping through my mom's voice at that moment could've melted the insulation off the speaker wires.

'That's not what I meant.'

Mom found some invisible point off-camera and stared at it. 'What was she saying about getting out of here tomorrow?'

194

'I have no idea.'

'You acted like it meant something to you.'

Dad shook his head. 'I was trying to get her to tell us something. Anything. Maybe about Perry.'

Mom straightened, looked back at him. 'You think they have him somewhere?'

'I don't know.'

'Would she tell you, if you asked?'

'Probably not.'

'You should try.'

'All right.'

'He doesn't even have a passport anymore,' my mom said, and she sounded like she was going to start crying again. 'He doesn't have anything.'

'I'll see what I can find out when she comes back. But you have to believe me, Julie, as God is my witness, there was never anything between me and that woman.'

Mom didn't say anything for a long time. When she finally did, her voice was cold and distant.

'I agree,' she said.

'You do?'

'About the fact that it doesn't matter right now,' she

clarified. 'Right now I just hope Perry's all right.'

Dad looked at her, but she didn't say anything else.

The clip ended there.

30

'Timebomb' – Beck

I stood perfectly still behind Erich, staring at the screen. The funny thing about equilibrium is that you don't realize how much you rely on it until something comes along and yanks it out from under you. Somewhere in front of me, he was leaning forward, typing on the keyboard, little clicks adding up to something, or nothing, at the moment, I really didn't care. I barely felt Gobi's hand on my shoulder.

'I am sorry, Perry. Your father – '

'Yeah.' I turned, or at least my legs decided to, taking the rest of me along for the ride. Suddenly I didn't want to talk about it. Talking about it meant thinking about it, and it didn't take too much thought to realize how easily Paula could have used my dad the way she'd used me, as a way of gathering information about Gobi, and earning his trust, until eventually he'd leave himself and his family vulnerable. I tried to imagine my dad resisting Paula's advances – I wanted to visualize him pushing her away, saying how wrong it was, she was dating his son. How he could never do something like that. There was wrong, and there was *wrong*, and there was this.

But I knew him too well.

And Gobi did too.

I tried to make my voice as calm as possible. 'How much more time until you can pinpoint where this was sent from?'

'Not much longer,' Erich said, clicking in a new set of commands and watching the screen flash back at him. 'They're somewhere in western Europe. I'll have the location soon. We may have to wait a few more minutes.'

'That's okay,' I said. 'Now I really do want to hit something.'

The plank in Gobi's hands was three inches thick and just wide enough for me to picture my dad's face on it. I watched it turn into Armitage's, then Paula's, then back to my dad's, then a screwball combination of the three. I curled my fingers into a fist. With every second I waited, I could feel the desire to lash out and punch it building up inside me, all the way from my shoulder down my arm until it had formed a buzzing electrical current.

Erich stood next to me, his voice patient and unhurried. 'With tae kwon do,' he said, 'the key is to aim at a point beyond your target, so that you are actually punching *through* it. In order to break that board, your hand will have to be traveling about thirty feet per second when it makes contact. Think of your fist as a bullet fired from a gun. Visualize it passing through the board. Are you ready?'

I nodded, checked my stance, and made a fist, cocking one knuckle out slightly like he'd shown me. I could feel the blood pounding in my temples. Putting all the force of my body into the punch, I swung at the block of wood. There was a sharp *thwack* as my knuckles smashed into it, and a bright bolt of pain ricocheted back up my arm to my shoulder, where it erupted into a throb of pure agony. I doubled over, clutching my hand and trying not to pass out or pee myself.

'You are not focused.' Erich's voice floated in from far outside the pain. 'Anger is not focus.'

'Yeah,' I managed. 'Thanks.'

'Check your pulse.'

I put the fingertips of my good hand to the side of my neck. It was throbbing almost too fast to count. I took deep breaths, willing myself to slow it down, until it was in the sixties.

'Try again.'

'No thanks.' I shook my head. 'That plank is unbreakable.'

Erich looked at Gobi again, then set his feet parallel with his shoulders. An expression of absolute focus, almost serenity, came over his face. I saw him draw back and swing his fist directly at the plank.

The whole wall exploded in front of us.

31

'Blow Up the Outside World' – Soundgarden

'RPG,' Erich shouted, his voice barely audible over the aftershock.

I scrambled backwards, and all the geek inside me could think was, *They're attacking us with role-playing games?*

Gobi shoved me out of the way as a wide sheet of orange flame erupted through the gym. Bits of plaster and shreds of steel and glass fragments drifted through on a bitter cold wind, and through the hole in the wall, I saw it was dark out. Night had fallen. There were no windows here, and until that moment, I'd had no idea what time of day it was.

Erich again: 'These outer walls are reinforced eighteen-centimeter steel. This is not supposed to happen.'

'Oh, shit.'

'Stay down.' Without bothering to glance back in my direction, he unlocked the wall rack of automatic weapons and started taking down what looked like an AK-47 and a banana clip of ammo, then jammed them together and tossed the loaded gun overhand across the room at Gobi. She caught it one-handed without so much as a backwards glance. Erich reached for the rack again and selected an even bigger machine gun for himself, snapped on the night-scope, then grabbed a pair of tactical vests and handed one to Gobi and held the other out to me. 'Put this on if you don't want to die.'

It sounded like a good plan, at least the not-dying part. I reached for the vest and almost dropped it, then pushed my arms through its webbing, feeling twenty pounds of high-impact synthetic polymer settle on my shoulders and neck like a yoke. Maybe that was how they saved your life – once you put it on, you'd never be able to leave home.

A second rocket-propelled grenade slammed into the already half-demolished gym with a lung-vibrating *BOOM,* this one coming directly up from below, and I felt my knees turn to Jell-O, shifting me off-balance. Somewhere to my left, a tall rack of barbells fell over, crashing against the floor, sending hundreds of pounds in weights rolling sideways toward the hole in the floor that hadn't even been there ten seconds earlier. Whoever was down there, I hope the weights landed right on top of him.

BOOM! A third blast, and all of Europe jumped and shook itself off like a wet dog. When my vision steadied I saw that Gobi and Erich had positioned themselves on either side of the hole in the wall, which was still actively blazing like a burning circus hoop about to spew a stream of Bengalese tigers. As if on cue, they both pivoted and started shooting down onto the street. I'd seen them square off against each other, but I hadn't seem them fighting together. It was like watching a soldier and his shadow moving at the same time in tight, concise, almost choreographed maneuvers. I couldn't tell if I was more grateful or jealous.

After emptying the first clip, Erich ducked back to reload, slinging a machine pistol over his shoulder, and I saw Gobi step in and fire off another thirty rounds into the darkness. For a second or two, everything was hugely, ear-ringingly silent. I couldn't see who was down there, but whoever it was seemed undeterred by the counterattack, because the third fusillade of grenades came harder than ever. From overhead I heard the shriek of splintered metal as the ceiling caved in over Erich's gleaming display of Samurai swords and masks.

Gobi threw me a coat. 'Time to go,' she shouted, while Erich took up his post at the wall.

'Why do I need a – '

'It's flame-repellent.'

I shoved my arms through the sleeves. 'Where are we going?'

'Down.'

'*What?*'

She grabbed me by the collar and we jumped through the hole in the floor. The twenty-foot drop turned gravity into a car crash, smashing us feet-first into the old wine shop, which was already on fire, empty glass bottles and wooden shelves splintering everywhere. Panic got me staggering to my feet, where I took in a lungful of smoke, doubled over, and suddenly forgot how to breathe, walk, or think properly.

'*Idiot!*' Gobi shouted. She made the word sound like an exciting new energy drink, something maybe mixed out of equal parts taurine and extreme annoyance. 'Where are you going?' Grabbing my arm from out of nowhere, she yanked me forward, my feet blundering through the debris. In the smoke, all I could see were chaotic splutters of automatic gunfire among the broken bottles, like a garden of strange orange and red flowers.

We fell backwards through a hole in the wall, coughing and choking out onto wet concrete.

'Come on.'

I stared up at the blazing skeleton of the storefront, dizzy from the fumes. My consciousness was already wavering in and out. 'What about Erich?'

'He will be fine.'

But she didn't sound like she meant it.

Don't black out, I told myself. *Just hold on.*

I tried to say something, and the world went dark.

32

'Wake Up' – Rage Against the Machine

'I'm here.' I lifted my head, cringing. 'You don't have to keep hitting me.'

'That is inside of car door.' Gobi's voice came from far away, drifting in from somewhere on the far side of Greenwich Mean Time. 'You keep knocking your face on it.'

'Oh.' My head cleared all at once, like a fogged windshield sliced across by wipers. I hadn't been unconscious, exactly, more like grayed out, a combination of carbon monoxide and a more than slightly heightened sense of reality, a kind of psychological altitude sickness. I realized that we were back inside one of Zermatt's little shuttles, rattling along the main drag at sixty miles an hour, except this time Gobi was the one steering it.

'How did they find us?'

'Matter of time.'

'Wait, you're *driving?*'

'I can drive.'

If this was true, it was only in the broadest sense of the word. She was careening wildly from side to side up the narrow street, jerking the steering wheel back and forth like she'd learned how to drive from one of those old movies where they apparently projected the background behind the actors' heads, blew air in their faces, and told them to steer.

Up in front of us, I saw dozens of lights filling the street, heard music and noise – a parade in progress now disrupted by the onset of World War Three. Gobi was aiming right toward it, one-handed, which allowed her to lean out the window and keep shooting at whoever was coming up behind us.

'Keep your head down.'

'Where are we going?'

She didn't answer, and her eyes got very wide. I tried to think of anything that could actually take her by surprise, but I didn't have to wonder for long. In front of us, hundreds of Bavarian Santa Clauses were standing in the street, watching the fire start to spread.

'What the hell . . . ?' I looked back up at the colorful banner dangling overhead and remembered what it had said – CLAUWAU. We'd arrived here in the middle of some kind of international Santa Claus convention.

There were Santas everywhere. Most of them looked as freaked out as I was, but in the chaos it was hard to tell. One of them spun around as we blasted past, and I wondered if Paula and whoever else was after us had the foresight to dress their assassins as Saint Nick. Another grenade erupted up from somewhere with a *WHOOSH* and a hiss, and a mob of men and women in red suits with pillows tucked underneath scattered in every direction. As the street finally started to clear, I saw one particular Santa, screaming, his beard on fire, running for the alley. Reindeer – real ones this time, having broken loose from their harness – went sprinting off after him in every direction. It was Santageddon.

Gobi swerved wildly around a second herd of Santas with matching Elvis pompadours and gold lamé boots that seemed just a few seconds earlier to have been scaling a tall wooden pole in some kind of contest. The pole had fallen over, and Gobi steered around it, thumping the car's left tires hard enough that I heard something snap off underneath us.

'Where are you going?' I managed.

The answer was 'Helipad.'

'When we get to top,' Gobi said, 'leave all talking to me.'

'You actually think they'll just let us fly out of here?'

'I think, yes.' She held the machine gun up, then jammed her hand into her coat, brought out a wad of euros in a big metal money clip, and shoved it in my hand. 'Hold on to this. In case we have to negotiate.'

'Isn't that what the gun's for?'

The question was rhetorical and we both knew it. We had arrived at our destination. I didn't realize it at the time, even when I looked up and saw the big blue and white AIR ZERMATT garage opening in front of us to reveal a drive-in elevator the size of an aircraft carrier.

We drove in and the elevator began to rise, the doors opening at the top, allowing us to roll out onto the roof.

The helicopter was waiting for us.

The fuselage was red with white call letters painted on the side. Its propellor was already running, making that unmistakable *pop-pop-pop* of the blades accompanied by the high-pitched whine of turbines. I'd read somewhere about Vietnam veterans who couldn't stand the sound of rotors because it gave them flashbacks to the war, and at that moment I totally understood. Even though it was half a world away, the second I heard that familiar sound and smelled the exhaust, it was like I was right back in midtown Manhattan, gunfire and shouting, exploding glass and broken promises on the forty-seventh floor.

I glanced back down at Zermatt spread out below us, sirens and fire at the far end of the street, where, from the sound of it, the battle of the Hotel Schoeneweiss was apparently still in progress. Up above it all, the mountains stood almost lost in the distance except for a few faint beacons, tiny lights at their peaks.

Gobi and I got out of the car just as the chopper's hatch opened.

The woman who stepped through it was familiar too.

'Hey, Stormaire,' Paula shouted across the helipad. She

was wearing a black knit ski cap and parka, and grinning like she'd just won the Big Air competition at the Winter X Games. Even from here, I could see the bruise on her face where Gobi had ax-kicked her back in Venice. 'Written any good songs lately?'

This time her pistol was pointed right at Gobi.

33

'Cold Hard Bitch' – Jet

For a second, nobody moved. We all just stood there, our clothes flapping like windsocks in the rushing air high above the lights of Zermatt.

Then I saw a red dot appear on Gobi's forehead, and traced it to a man in a long coat poised inside the helicopter, holding a rifle outfitted with a laser-scope, fifteen yards away. He was bald, with a long, almond-shaped face that tapered down to a trim silver-gray goatee, making him look vaguely satanic.

It took me a second to recognize him, but I made the connection soon enough. The last time I'd seen him he'd been wearing a priest's collar in the Grand Canal, when he'd come bursting out of the Louis Vuitton steamer trunk and opened his eyes, alive despite all the bullets that had been fired in his direction. Gobi's target, the one she'd failed to finish off. Right away I could tell that Gobi recognized him just by the subtle shift in her posture.

You should have killed him in Venice, I thought.

The man gave us both an amused glance, and in the chopper's interior lights I saw his lips tightening at the corners, like the spontaneous pucker of a time-lapse scar. I looked back at the red dot on Gobi's forehead. Counting the rifle and the pistol, she had at least two guns trained right on her, maybe more if Paula had another sniper waiting somewhere else. With the two of us standing out here exposed on the helipad, with all these mountains and rooftops around us, the idea didn't seem the least bit paranoid.

It had started snowing. White flakes began to drift down, little sugar-spun strands and helixes swirling almost weightlessly through the landing lights. Lit by the rifle's laser-scope, they looked downright magical.

'Paula,' I shouted over the helicopter's roar. 'Where's my family?'

'They're safe,' she said. 'For now.'

'Where?'

'You know, I was thinking maybe we should take some time apart.' Her eyes flicked to Gobi. 'See other people.' She gave a sympathetic shrug. 'It's not you, it's me.'

'Whatever you say.'

'Hey.' Paula wrinkled her nose at me. 'It was fun while it lasted, though, right?'

I glanced at Gobi. She'd turned her head so I couldn't see her expression, and even if I had, it would have been impossible to say what was going through her mind. She still had the machine gun from Erich's place, but I didn't know how much ammo she had left, and even if she was fully loaded, we were simply outgunned. She might have been able to take out one of the shooters, but not both of them, and that kevlar vest wasn't going to do any good against a headshot at fifteen yards.

'Once we're out of here with Gobi,' Paula shouted, 'you'll get a phone call. Your parents and your sister will be released unharmed.'

'What if I don't believe you?'

'Who says you have a choice?'

She had a point. It was snowing harder now, big fat flakes drifting down from the sky, clogging my eyelashes. I brushed them away and took in a deep, throat-aching breath of cold air.

'Who's in charge now that Armitage is dead?' I asked.

That adrenalized grin came blazing back again. How had I never noticed how white her teeth were before?

'That depends,' Paula said, 'on who ends up with Gobi.'

'What do you mean?'

Paula gazed appreciatively at Gobi. 'She's a human weapon, Stormaire. The best mercenary around. One in a million. Armitage seriously underestimated her capabilities, and it cost him his life. I won't make that mistake.'

'It's not like she's programmable,' I said. 'She's not just some machine that will do whatever you tell her.'

'I think she will, once she finds out what I'm offering.'

'And what's that?'

'Clearly more than you ever could.'

'She doesn't kill people for money, Paula.'

'You're standing up for her. How gallant.'

Throughout all of this, Gobi still hadn't said anything. Some part of me was just waiting for her to snap into motion, dodging bullets while she opened fire on Paula and the helicopter. Paula must have been waiting for it too. The grin disappeared and her eyes went cold, and when she spoke again her voice was both louder and sharper, an announcement of ultimatum marking the close of play.

'Gobija Zaksauskas,' Paula said.

Gobi didn't budge.

'This is the situation. If your next move is anything except putting down that gun and coming with me now, Perry's whole family is going to die in the most horrible way that you can imagine.' Paula kept the gun pointed straight at her. 'Let me repeat that. Either you come with us now, or I will kill Perry and his family. Is there anything about this scenario that you don't understand?'

Nobody spoke. I realized that I was holding my breath. We all knew the stakes. If there was one miracle left in the night, I prayed for it to happen now.

Gobi raised the machine gun, turned, and looked at me.

'*As atsiprasau,*' she said. 'I am sorry, Perry.'

'Wait,' I said. 'Just – '

Behind the pistol, Paula tensed, getting ready. I saw the bald sharpshooter on the helicopter coil tighter around his rifle. The red dot on Gobi's head held perfectly still between her eyes, the punctuation mark that waits for all of us somewhere in the end.

But Gobi just put down her weapon on the tarmac and walked over to the helicopter. She got onboard without a backwards glance.

It lifted up and flew away, leaving me standing there alone.

34

'I Will Buy You a New Life' – Everclear

A half-hour later I found myself back in the center of town. The fire was finally out at the Hotel Schoeneweiss, leaving Main Street smelling like the biggest ashtray on the planet. Everywhere I looked, dozens of scorched and blinking Santa Clauses were still roaming the streets, dazed and bewildered, and the singed ClauWau banner was dangling from one of the buildings. Blue flashing police and fire truck lights flickered off the blackened foundation of the old liquor store, which had already been cordoned off by emergency crews. An upside-down sleigh lay half buried under a pile of bricks. A reindeer dipped its head to drink from a black puddle with a Santa cap floating in it.

Everywhere I looked, Swiss cops and soldiers stood with high-intensity LED flashlights, shining them on the faces of passersby, lining up eyewitnesses against the wall, asking for ID.

I turned and slunk up the other way, down an alley, and disappeared into the darkness.

I took the wad of euros that Gobi had given me out of my pocket and counted them with only slightly shaking hands. There was a few hundred here, along with the fake ID that she'd given me back in Italy, a picture snapped at a train station photo booth, a face I barely recognized as mine. I could get on another train, if I had the slightest idea where to go.

Or I could just give up. Wave the white flag. Sweet surrender. It had never been more tempting. Even if I could get my family back again, what would life back in America be like? Was 'normal and ordinary' still any kind of option? Had it ever been?

A clumsy, scraping splash rang down from the far end of the alley. I heard a muffled curse and a series of slowly approaching footsteps.

Halfway down the alley, the man switched on a flashlight, and I saw his face.

The beard.

The sneer.

The camera.

There was no mistaking that combination – Swierczynski.

He was wearing a long, shabby coat with tails that practically dragged the ground behind him so that they picked up little scraps of debris along the way, which was probably his idea of going undercover. I could tell by the way he was moving that he hadn't seen me yet.

I felt a surge of adrenaline – it felt good to be mad about something I could do something about right away. I might not know the first thing about fighting, but at this point, I didn't care what happened to me, and that alone gave me the advantage.

Edging back into the shadows, I put my back to the wall and waited, hearing his boots shuffle closer, waiting until he was right in front of me. I remembered back in Venice when he'd tried to grab Gobi's gun. He hadn't been particularly quick about it – without the element of surprise, he had no advantage at all.

I reached out, grabbed the camera by the strap, and twisted.

He grunted and went down, already on his back by the time my knee landed on his chest.

'Still trying to tail Gobi?' I got right into his face, close enough that I could smell the pickles and sour vodka on his breath. Whatever Kaya was paying this guy, it was too much. 'I might be able to help you with that.'

'Where is she?'

I climbed off his chest. 'Let's go.'

'Where?'

'On your feet,' I said. 'We're going to see Kaya.'

He blinked at me, not understanding.

'Right now,' I said. 'It's time to visit your boss.'

A quick, dismissive head shake. 'Is not possible.'

'Oh, is possible.' I gave him a cold smile that had nothing to do with any of the ordinary reasons that people smile – happiness, humor, hope. 'If there's one thing I've learned in my tour of Europe, it's that as human beings, we're all a whole lot more flexible than we might think.'

'But I cannot – '

'I want to talk to Kaya. You have a contact number, an e-mail . . . You tell him I want a meeting right now, tonight.'

'I cannot make promises.' He was sounding more

Slavic by the moment. 'Is not my decision to make.'

'Ask yourself how pissed off Kaya's going to be when he finds out that you lost Gobi,' I told him. 'She was working for him, right? And you're supposed to be her babysitter. In other words, you had one job and you screwed it up. How much of your ass do you think he's going to chew off for losing her in Switzerland?' I waited, silently counting to ten before adding, almost off-handedly, 'Especially when I can tell him where to find her?'

He recrossed his arms and glared at me even harder, then muttered something in Russian.

Twenty minutes later, we were on a train.

35

'This Is Not America' – David Bowie

There was a car waiting for us at the Lausanne train station, a gunmetal blue Peugeot 306. Its driver never said a word as he drove us out of the lot and into the Alpine night. Through tinted glass, I watched snowcapped peaks and summits slide past us in a darkly winding blur of ear-popping dips and hairpin turns, the driver hardly slowing, barely steering, as if the car knew the way by itself. Slouched in the back beside me, Swierczynski brooded in morose eastern European silence, breathing audibly through his beard and doing everything in his power to make the expensive leather upholstery smell like a Ukrainian deli. I would have been okay with opening one of the windows, except that the wind was really howling outside and it felt like it was getting colder by the minute.

I stared out at the dark mountains.

I thought about my family.

I thought about Gobi.

Of course, my bluff about being able to tell him where she was had been exactly that, a bluff. But I'd gotten out of tighter spots with guys more dangerous than him, and in the end, he couldn't afford to be wrong about me, even if it was a long shot.

After an hour of driving we came down into a small Swiss village with narrow cobblestone streets and tall church steeples rising up on either side. It was almost midnight, and the whole town seemed asleep or deserted. This place, whatever it was called, made Zermatt look like Manhattan by comparison. The Peugeot stopped in front of a little corner tavern with a few lights burning inside, and Swierczynski got out and gestured for me to follow him.

Halfway through the doorway, I stopped him.

'If this is a setup,' I said, 'you'll never see her again. You know that, right?'

He grunted like he didn't particularly care about that

part anymore and held the door, ushering me the rest of the way inside.

The tavern was sawdusty and desolate, a drafty old-world beer hall with deer and mountain-goat heads stuffed and mounted on the walls above a dartboard that no one was using. At the far end of the room, long wooden tables sat in front of a roaring fire. The bartender glanced up at me for the briefest of seconds, then ducked behind a row of taps to finish polishing the stein in front of him with the determined air of a proprietor who knew when to mind his own business.

I looked across the room to where a man in a suit was sitting by himself in front of the fire with a glass of wine. For a second we just looked at each other. Usually when you describe someone, you say he was in his forties, or had silver hair or a pointed nose or whatever. But the thing about this guy was, the longer I looked at him, the less sure I was about any defining physical feature. He could have been twenty-nine or forty-six. In the firelight, his hair might have been gray, or light blond, or even silver-streaked black. The only things that really stood out were the cold indifference radiating from his eyes, and that sense of anonymity that, in itself, was deeply chilling.

'Kaya,' I said.

He snorted. A smile that wasn't a smile twisted like a thin wire at the corner of his mouth, and he took a business card out of his pocket and handed it to me. It read:

```
William J. Nolan
Support Integrations Officer
Central Intelligence Agency
```

'Kaya,' I said, and looked back down at the card. 'CIA. Nice touch.'

'Believe it or not,' Nolan said, 'it started out as a speech-enabled text error. Hard *C*, then *I, A*. The original program didn't recognize acronyms. In the end, we kept it that way. Kind of a if-it's-not-broke-why-fix-it sort of deal.'

I don't know why I was surprised. 'So the CIA are the ones running Gobi?'

'Gobi,' he said. 'That's cute. What's she call you – Pokey?'

'You know she goes by that name.'

'Yes,' Nolan said, 'but I prefer Zusane Elzbieta Zaksauskas.' He brought out a thick folder and opened it on the table, next to his wineglass. Inside I saw whole stacks of black-and-white photos, handwritten reports, official documents, and photocopied receipts stapled together, flickering in the firelight from behind us. There were a few pictures of me in there as well, surveillance pictures from our night in New York. Nolan flipped past them without comment until he reached a page of vital statistics. 'Born September twenty-third, 1988, Karmelava, Lithuania, twenty-four years old, various aliases, weapons and combat training, blah-blah-blah, whereabouts currently unknown.'

'I know where she is.'

'Right.' Nolan hardly raised an eyebrow. 'Not to burst your bubble, junior, but you'll forgive me if I don't jump right up and offer to buy you a drink for that information on the spot.'

I frowned. 'So . . . what? If you don't think I can help you, why did you agree to meet me?'

'First rule of poker, kid. Look around the table for a sucker. If you don't see him, it's you.'

'I've already figured that out.'

'In fact, the only reason you're even sitting here tonight is that I wanted to be sure you actually exist. You know, they have a running bet on you back at Langley? None of the analysts could believe one guy could have such spectacularly shitty luck with women.'

He tossed another surveillance photo across the table and gave me plenty of time to look at this one. It was a shot of me and Paula from early October, walking hand in hand outside Film Forum in New York. We'd just come out of a showing of *The Getaway,* the 1972 Sam Peckinpah original with Ali MacGraw and Steve McQueen. The picture had been taken just as I was leaning in to kiss her, and the camera had captured a look of supremely idiotic happiness on my face. If I survived this, I secretly pledged that I'd never let myself be that happy again.

'Paula Daniels, age twenty-four,' Nolan said, 'born Paula Monash, an American citizen who grew up in Dubai.' Paula was twenty-four? And Monash? I was still looking at the picture, trying to figure out where I'd heard that name before, as Nolan kept talking.

'Paula's father, Everett Monash, was an American financier working alongside George Armitage in the UAE. She turned eighteen and got into the family business.'

'She told me her dad was a record producer.'

Nolan was in the process of sipping wine and almost snorted it out his nose. 'My. God.' He coughed and cleared his throat. 'How is it you are still alive?'

I looked at the crime scene picture from yesterday – or was it two days ago? – of Armitage's body splayed across the Venetian piazza in a pile of broken glass and spilled wine. Even in black and white it was pretty gruesome, like a big pan of lasagna had fallen on him.

'Why did you have Gobi kill him?'

'If you're asking why we picked Zaksauskas for the job, you of all people should know that. The girl's born to kill. If you're asking why we targeted Armitage . . .' Nolan steepled his fingers in front of his lips, parsing information carefully. 'Let's just say that he and his checkered past presented a problem that our government couldn't afford to deal with publicly – and he did need to be dealt with. We're talking about a guy who helped sell Stinger missiles to Kurdish separatists for pocket change, and now he thinks he's Richard Branson? Sorry, no. So back in August, one of our analysts happened to read that college essay you wrote online, and your crazy little European chick seemed like a perfect bet for cleanup duty.'

'Wait.' A wave of nausea rolled over me, and I suddenly felt sick to my stomach. 'You picked Gobi because of me?'

'It was a great essay, kid. Vivid prose. Felt like I was there.' He must have seen my face, because he shook his head. 'Hey, don't beat yourself up about it. You didn't know. Once she takes care of Paula, we'll be all finished with her.'

'You know she's got my family.'

Nolan went quiet, all smugness gone. *What?*

'Paula. She's got my parents and my sister.'

'As of when?'

'Yesterday at least. Paula had pictures of them on her iPad, in some room somewhere.'

'You're sure that she's the one who did it?'

'If she didn't, she's associated with whoever did.'

'You have any proof?'

'I told you,' I said, 'I saw the picture. There's a video file too, where my mom and dad are talking about her.'

'You have that file?'

'No. It was on her iPad.'

'And where's the iPad?'

'It got blown up in Zermatt.'

Nolan grunted. 'I've noticed that happens a lot when Zusane Zaksauskas is around.'

'We're talking about my family,' I said. 'My parents. And my sister. Why would I possibly make something like that up?'

He didn't bother answering the question. 'And you have no idea where they might be?'

'Somewhere in western Europe. They're in a room with no windows and no furniture. Other than that, no.'

'Well' – Nolan didn't look happy – 'we'll look into it.' Even he must have realized how lame that sounded, because he straightened his posture and attempted to rephrase the statement. 'We'll make it a top priority. Meanwhile, we've got a tight hold on the asset, so everything's stable, for now at least. Once she takes care of Paula, she'll be back.'

'The asset?' It took me a second to figure out what he was talking about. 'Are you talking about Gobi?'

'Who else?'

'You're talking about her like she's some kind of brain-washed sleeper agent.'

Nolan snorted. 'Kid, you've been watching too many movies.'

'Then how can you be so sure she'll be back?'

'Money isn't the only reason people do things.' Nolan shrugged. 'Our doctors give her eight to twelve months tops.'

I stared at him. For a second the tavern around us was so quiet that all I could hear was the fire snapping and popping in the hearth.

'What?'

Nolan's eyebrows twitched. For the second time, he looked interested in the conversation.

'What, you didn't know?'

And he showed me the last item in his folder.

36

'Bullet with Butterfly Wings' – The Smashing Pumpkins

I'd never seen an MRI image before, but I recognized a human brain when I saw one. Nolan pointed to a white spot toward the front of the picture, just above the eyeballs.

'Glioblastoma multiforme,' he said, 'stage three. Temporal lobe, they say. Aggressive as shit, the way I understand it.'

Looking at that little spot, no bigger than a dime, I thought back to Swierczynski, what he'd said back in Venice:

The bullet is already in your brain.

'Apparently she'd had cancer once before,' Nolan said, 'as a child, in the thyroid. Surgeons tried to remove it back in Lithuania, I guess, with a thyroidectomy, but they kind of botched the job.' Another shrug. This guy was turning out to be the world heavyweight champion of shruggers. 'Eastern European medicine . . . what are you going to do?'

I thought of the scar across her throat, the one that Erich had mentioned to me back in Zermatt. I wanted to say something, anything, but all the moisture seemed to have disappeared from my mouth.

'But this puppy?' Nolan tapped the white spot on the MRI. 'Going to be a whole lot trickier. I'm told there's maybe five or six neurosurgeons in the world who can get it out without permanent brain damage, and even then . . .'

'And you promised her the operation if she took care of Armitage for you.'

'I told her what I had to.'

'What about now?'

'That's the beauty of it.' Nolan grinned, and took another sip of his wine, which was almost gone. 'She's not our problem anymore. See how everything works out? That's what makes America the greatest country in the world.'

Before I knew what I was doing, I grabbed the table and flipped it over, sending it forward with a splintering crash.

Papers, photographs, and the bottle and glass all hit the floor. Nolan jumped up, and when he looked back to me, it was with the startled unease of a man who'd just discovered that the dog he'd been taunting wouldn't just bark but might actually jump up and bite.

'There's no need to get bitchy, kid. We'll figure out what's going on with your family – I already told you that. Twenty-four hours or less, we'll get a phone call, bring 'em out all smiles and do the CNN shuffle.' He pointed at me with a big blunt finger. 'Don't piss in the wind on this one.'

'You owe her,' I said.

'Shit.'

'You made her a promise.'

Nolan studied me for a moment. Some of the intensity lifted from his face, and when he spoke again, his voice was different, almost earnest – suddenly he was a man who genuinely believed what he was saying and wanted to be understood.

'Let's get something straight, Perry. I told you before, Zusane Zaksauskas is a born predator. She's a dirty bomb with a pulse. It's what she is – and it's *all* she is. If she wasn't doing this for us, she'd be doing it for somebody else.' He blinked, all watery-eyed and sympathetic, like maybe there was still a way that we could all walk away friends. 'I've got kids of my own, all right? Two beautiful girls – they live with their mom back in Virginia. Amazing young women. They play violin and ride dressage. Someday they're going to grow up and go to college and raise kids of their own and live long, happy lives.' His expression fell. 'But somebody like this?' He looked at the Gobi file, scattered around his feet. 'I don't mean to sound callous, but short of a bullet to the head – cancer's the best thing for it.'

I stared at him. 'You're a real asshole, you know that?'

There must have been something threatening in my voice, because I saw a second man standing up in the corner of the room, where I hadn't noticed him until now. Without taking his eyes off me, Nolan gestured for the other agent to sit down.

'It's okay, Jeff,' he said. 'Kid's emotional, that's all. The teenage years.'

'I'm not emotional,' I said, and saying those words aloud, I realized it was true. I had finally remembered where I'd heard the name Monash before, and I felt calmer than I had in days. If I'd put my fingers to my carotid artery, I would've felt my heart rate running a steady sixty beats per minute, maybe even slower. 'Let me see those pictures again.'

Grudgingly: 'Which ones?'

'Of Paula, when she was little.'

With another almost indiscernible shrug, Nolan squatted down and picked up the papers that I'd spilled when I'd dumped the table. After gathering them up, he shoved them in my direction so that I could sort through them. Here she was standing in the Dubai Hilton with her nanny; here she was in Paris, walking along among the chestnut trees on the Avenue des Champs-Élysées toward the Arc de Triomphe with a pretty blond woman that I recognized from framed photos in Paula's apartment as her mother. When I got to the next one, I stopped.

'This was her dad?'

'Everett Monash, yeah. The one that Gobi hit outside the train station, before Armitage.'

I looked at the snapshot. Paula, probably six or seven at the time, was sitting on his shoulders in Piazza San Marco, in front of the cathedral where we'd just stood two days ago. I looked at Paula's young, smooth face, and then down at Everett's – a tall, vaguely satanic-looking bald man with a trim goatee that looked very similar to how I'd seen it earlier tonight, when he'd been sitting in the helicopter – the man who had been pointing the rifle at Gobi. The man I'd first seen bursting out of a steamer trunk in the Grand Canal.

I pointed down at his face. 'He was Gobi's first Venice target?'

'That's right. Monash. He and Paula were part of Armitage's organization.'

'You know he's still alive, right?'

Nolan's eyes widened just a millimeter. 'Bullshit.'

'It's true,' I said. 'He and Paula have Gobi right now. And they seem to think they can turn her to their side.' I looked at him. 'You better hope she believed you when you lied about getting her that surgery, Agent Nolan – or I don't think you'll ever see her again.'

'You're lying about Monash. We got independent confirmation that Gobi shot him and dropped his body in the canal.'

'Yeah,' I said, 'and who do you think was in that canal with him when he opened his eyes?'

'Word of advice, kid. Don't shit a shitter.' Nolan grabbed back his files, shuffled them away, then picked up his coat and slipped it on, all business now. 'Here's the deal. You're going to let Jeff here drive you back to the embassy, and you're going to sit there like a good boy and let us do our job, and nobody's going to mention anything about Zusane Zaksauskas ever again. Got it?'

'Sure,' I said. 'There's just one problem.'

Now he just sounded tired. 'What's that?'

'I don't trust you to save my family. I don't think you know half of what *you* think you know.' I pointed straight at him. 'And I definitely don't trust the CIA to do anything more than what serves its own purpose to help me out of here.' I looked back over at the guy who'd stood up when I'd called Nolan an asshole. 'And that means that whatever arrangement you might have planned with Gobi, I'm about twelve hours from pulling the whole thing down on your heads in the most publicly humiliating way possible.'

Nolan turned red, then purple. His fists tightened at his sides, clenched and pink and somehow anal. On the satisfaction scale, it wasn't quite on par with watching him try to pass a kidney stone, but it was close.

'You smart-ass little punk, what makes you think – ' He stopped himself mid-rant, and his whole face went stone cold, all trace of emotion gone, all at once. 'You do not want to get involved in this, Perry. I promise you. I will make your life hell.'

'Too late,' I said.

In my pocket, something began to vibrate.

37

'Don't Let Me Explode' – The Hold Steady

Nolan had already turned and started walking away. 'You ready to go?' he asked, angling toward the door.

I slipped my hand into the pocket of the heavy winter parka that Gobi had tossed me back at Erich's and felt the small rectangular shape vibrating inside. After sneaking out the cell phone that I hadn't known was there, I flipped it on and glanced at the three-word message on the screen.

men's room now

I dropped the phone back in my pocket. 'I gotta hit the bathroom before we go.'

Nolan gave me a distrustful glance. 'It's cold and dark out there, kid. Don't do anything stupid.'

'Don't worry.' On the way past the bar, I brushed past Swierczynski, who'd been sitting there with a thick mug of coffee, to the heavy wooden door marked HERREN. In the background I heard Nolan's voice continuing to warn me not to be stupid.

I swung the door open. The men's room was freezing cold, and right away I saw why. The window was wide open and Gobi was standing in front of me with a thick slab of wood in her hands. For a second all I could do was stare at her in shock.

'You are late.'

'Gobi, how – '

She pushed past me and jammed the wooden beam against the door, wedging it into the tiles and blocking it shut from the inside.

'Crawl through window.'

'What happened to the – '

'No talking.' She boosted me through the open window and out into the darkness, where I fell straight down into a pile of flattened cardboard boxes and bags of trash. A cat squalled and took off running. Gobi, having crawled through and dropped down after me, took my hand and yanked me up onto my feet. As we ran around to the front of the restaurant, I heard voices from inside, Nolan and the bartender and good old Swierczy, shouting, coughing, hammering on the door. There was an ice machine pushed in front of the main entrance, blocking it shut, and thick smoke oozing from the slight gap, but the door wasn't opening any farther than that.

I looked up at the roof.

'You blocked the chimney?'

'Watch out.' She pointed at the unconscious body of the driver sprawled on the ground next to the Peugeot, then opened the driver's-side door. 'You can still drive stick, yes?'

I got in and started the engine.

38

'Needle Hits E' – Sugar

'We have to talk,' I said.

She pointed out the intersection up ahead, where a rectangular yellow sign read MULHOUSE, FR – 50 KM. 'Turn left here.'

'How did you escape from Paula?'

'Is not far from here. Roads are clear.' She checked her watch.

'How did you find me?' I looked down at the phone that she'd dropped in my pocket. 'Does this thing have a GPS tracking beacon on it or something?'

She closed her eyes and sat back as if she hadn't heard me.

'Are you even going to answer me?'

She didn't move. The Peugeot's tires hugged the road, its high-performance engine barely making a sound above the low, steady whir of precision engineering. My hands tightened on the wheel and I checked to make sure we were both wearing our seat belts. Coming around the next bend, I swung to the side of the road and slammed the brakes hard enough to make her sit up straight and stare at me. Her face was taut and strained, and the glare in her eyes could have smelted pig iron.

'That asshole back at the restaurant told me everything,' I said. 'I know about . . .' Even then, as upset as I was, I couldn't make myself say the words *your brain tumor.* 'What's happening to you.'

Gobi just kept glaring at me. Her silence was a void, like no other silence in the world. It seemed to collapse inward, sucking all other sound into it, like the aural equivalent of a black hole. For a long moment we just sat there, facing each other like the last two people in Switzerland.

'Is nothing,' she murmured.

'Bullshit.'

'Is epilepsy.'

'Bullshit.'

'Who tells you these things? Kaya?' She snapped a glance back in the direction that we'd come. 'They lie.'

'Gobi, I saw the images of your brain.'

'And of course medical pictures cannot ever be altered. Images doctored. Different names put on.'

'If they're lying, then why were you working for them?'

She stared at the window, and I felt my heart race harder, like a gallon jug glugging out its contents into the hole at the bottom of my chest. I didn't realize until that moment how much I'd been hoping for another explanation, any explanation, hoping for anything besides what Nolan alleged to be true. Partly because I'd already decided that Gobi was the only way that I was going to save my family, but also because Gobi was Gobi. She was twenty-four years old. She belonged in the world – if not my world, than at least some version of it, somewhere.

'Look,' I said. 'I know that guy Nolan promised you the operation if you took care of Armitage and Monash and Paula. He told me all about it.'

'Is not for you to worry.'

'Oh, okay, I'll just stop. I'll just switch off my worrier.' I reached for her hand, and she jerked away as if I'd given her a shock. 'You know what, if you can't stand me so much, why the hell did you even bother coming back for me?'

'You would not survive five minutes on your own.'

I felt a quick sting of anger. 'Yeah, well, meet me in a year from now and we'll see who's doing better.'

She stiffened, drawing in a sharp breath, then exhaled with a little shudder and looked at me. The shadows across her face made it hard to see her expression, but her eyes gleamed around the rims in the light of the dashboard.

'Look, I'm sorry,' I said. 'That was harsh. I didn't mean it to come out like that.'

'You are doctor, Perry, yes? Go to medical school?'

'No.'

'But you are genius, yes? Smart American boy, you can see everything, you know what is right for everybody else?'

'Gobi – '

'You want to worry about someone, worry about yourself, falling in love with some rich girl who would sleep with your father to get what she wanted.'

'Don't even go there.'

She spat out something, a curse in Lithuanian that didn't require any translation. 'Just drive.'

I took my hands off the wheel. 'Forget it.'

'What?'

'I'm trying to help you,' I snapped. 'Don't you get that? I'm the only one that you can actually trust.'

Gobi glared at me. For a second I couldn't tell if she was going to take a swing at me or shove me out of the car. Then her chin trembled and her whole expression quivered and she started to laugh.

I stared at her. 'Now what?'

'I forgot how funny you are when you get mad.' She wrinkled up her forehead, lowering her voice, transforming it into an annoyingly accurate imitation of mine. *I am trying to help you, don't you get that? I am only one that you can actually trust.*

'Okay, first of all, I don't sound like that – '

'I will just turn my worrier off.'

'You're not funny.'

'Don't go there.'

'You're insane.'

'You're insane.'

I glared at her smirking back at me, then changed my own voice into a stiffly accented version of English.

'*Is not for you to worry about,*' I said.

She tilted her head slightly to one side. 'Is that supposed to be me?'

'*I am Gobi,*' I intoned. '*I am Goddess of Fire. I kill everything.*'

She shoved me. 'Shut up, stupid ass. That is not how I talk.'

'*No more Perry Stormaire bool-shit.*'

'Your essay is all wrong,' she said. 'All the talking that I do in your writing is wrong.'

I looked at her. 'You read my essay?'

Gobi nodded. 'Of course I read. On the Internet.'

'What did you think, aside from your dialogue?'

'It was – all right.' She looked up, tucking a strand of hair behind her ear. 'Some good parts.'

'Yeah, like what?'

'Like . . . when we kissed in that coffee house in Brooklyn. And when we danced together at the hotel on Central Park. Those parts I like.'

'You mean before you pulled that knife on me?'

'You liked it.'

'Oh, I liked it?'

'Yes, I think – yes.'

I reached out to her again, put my hand up along her temple, and this time she let me keep it there. I could feel the blood pumping in her veins, and tried not to think about what else was going on in there, growing inside her skull, but when her eyes flicked to me, I knew she'd already picked up my thoughts.

'How bad is it?' I asked.

She hesitated, and when she spoke again her voice was low and soft, not much more than a whisper. 'At first, you know, it was not so terrible. Even when I was training with Erich for the first time, three years ago? There was headaches at night, yes, and sometimes . . .' – she opened her mouth, mimed throwing up – 'in morning, you know? Then later came the shaking, the . . .'

'The seizures.'

'Yes.' She moved her head up and down, almost too slowly to be a nod. 'When I first came to live with you and your family. Neurologists, the first ones, they had said yes, is temporal lobe epilepsy, gave me medicine? But I think even then they knew. Because of before.'

'Your other cancer.'

She nodded, unconsciously touching the thin white scar on her throat, then reaching up to her head. 'But is worse, this.'

'When did you know for sure?'

'About the tumor?' She paused. 'After that night in New York. That man back there, Nolan. Approached me at the airport in Amsterdam. Told me what they wanted. They did blood work and MRI, and told me I could have surgery, if I . . .'

'If you did what they wanted.'

She nodded.

'And you believed them.'

She looked at me. 'What choice?'

The question hung between us, a riddle without an answer, maddening in its simplicity. We sat there in the darkness for what felt like eons, and I looked out at the road in front of us. It was absolutely silent. When I turned to face her again, I realized that she'd never stopped looking at me.

'How did you get out of that helicopter, anyway?'

'I jumped.'

'You jumped.'

'Yes.'

'Out of a helicopter.'

An edge of impatience now: 'I am the one with the brain damage, Perry. Are you an idiot?'

'What, like with a parachute?'

Sigh. 'After liftoff I went for the gun. Was not so difficult in enclosed space.' She shrugged. 'Pilot took a bullet in the head. Paula and her father and me . . . all grabbed parachutes. They got away before I could kill them.'

'Or they could kill you.'

She smiled wryly. 'They still thought that I will work for them as an assassin, if they get me to a surgeon and take care of this.' She touched her head. 'But I will stay with Kaya's offer.'

'You can't trust Kaya either.'

'Perry, you must promise me.'

'What?'

'Because of what is in my head, I sometimes . . . lose myself. Become confused. I know this is true. Erich told me that when you and I were in Switzerland – '

'Forget about it.'

'If that ever happens, and I – I put you in harm's way, you must promise you will end it cleanly.'

'What,' I said. 'You mean, break up with you?'

'Shut up.' She punched me. 'I am serious.'

'Ouch! Shit!'

'Your family was very kind to me when I was in America, Perry. They gave me a home, a safe place to stay so that I could finish what I had to do.' She looked at me slowly and I realized that she had already made up her mind. 'Do you want them back?'

'My family? You know I do.'

'We cannot go to police.' She opened her coat and I saw the gun that she'd taken from Paula on the helicopter, a nine-millimeter Glock semi-automatic. 'Not now.'

'No,' I said.

'What would you be willing to do?'

'Whatever it takes.'

'Do you remember how it was for us in New York that night?'

I nodded.

'And you are ready to go to war again?'

'If we have to.'

Gobi took out the sheet of paper, unfolded it, and told me what she had in mind. When she finished talking, the silence came back, filling the car again, and this time the quiet felt right and easy between us and I knew it was there to stay. I took in a breath and let it out, and eased my foot back on the gas, following the road through the forest of the night.

39

'I Am the Highway' – Audioslave

'You are ready?'

It was just after dawn. We were somewhere in France, gassing up the Peugeot at a BP station, steam rising off the cups of espresso that Gobi had brought out a few minutes earlier along with a loaf of bread. On the opposite side of the road, two cows were gazing at us with unblinking bovine indifference. If American cows looked bored, French cows had elevated it to an art form.

I started the engine, pulling away from the service station while Gobi tore a chunk of bread off, smeared it with cheese, and handed it to me. I wasn't hungry, but after driving through the night, I was starting to get the shakes. All around us, the countryside spilled out in wet brown fields that looked like the Cézanne paintings I'd seen in one of my mother's coffee table books. None of it looked like it had changed much in the last hundred years except for the occasional satellite dish.

My phone started to buzz. The one that Gobi had planted on me. I looked over at her.

'Who else has this number?'

'No one.'

I hit TALK. 'Hello?'

'Hey, kid.'

That voice, like broken gravel being shoveled in my ear. 'Agent Nolan,' I said, feeling Gobi react beside me as I glanced over my shoulder at the empty roadway behind us.

'Listen, about last night, no hard feelings, huh?' Nolan coughed, not bothering to cover his mouth. 'I didn't want you to think I was mad about that or anything.'

'That's a load off,' I said.

'You have to admit, it was kind of stupid, though, right?' This time the cough sounded more like a humorless chuckle, and it was easy to imagine him sitting in a safe house somewhere back in Switzerland, stirring Nescafé and checking his e-mail. 'You don't have many friends in Europe now.'

'I've got one.'

'I wanted to let you know that we checked on your family. Nothing yet.'

'Thanks, and good luck tracing this phone. I'm ditching it.'

'I would expect nothing less.'

'Goodbye, Nolan.'

'See you, Perry.'

As soon as he hung up, Gobi looked at me. 'What did he say?'

'He said I don't have many friends in Europe.'

'Is he right?'

I looked at the sign up ahead. PARIS – 262 KM.

'We'll see.'

40

'The Metro' – Berlin

By early afternoon we'd reached the outskirts of Paris and abandoned the Peugeot in a commuter lot at Joinville-le-Pont. I bought us two twenty-four-hour rail passes while Gobi wiped the car down, getting our prints off the wheel and the door handles. When the RER pulled up to the platform, we got onboard and took two seats in the very back.

Gobi leaned her head on my shoulder and dozed. People got on and off the train without noticing us. Outside it was raining again, big fat metal-colored droplets streaking the glass as we rocked past industrial parkways, warehouses, and factories outside the city. Power lines swooped and dipped like sine waves outside the window. A half-hour later, we changed from the commuter rail to the Metro, and I saw oil-slick puddles and landfills along the tracks, abandoned furniture, tangles of graffiti along the trestles, getting thicker and more elaborate, American words and hip-hop slang mixed in with French phrases and local iconography. If this wasn't Paris, we were definitely headed into New Jersey.

'Look.' She pointed out the window. 'Eiffel Tower.'

I stared at it rising above the brown and white rooftops. Until that moment I hadn't really registered where we were. For a while the buildings of Paris could have been the same anonymous tenements of any other city, apartments and drugstores with rain sluicing off the canopies, but as the train rose up on an elevated track, I saw the cathedrals and the river, and then we were in the middle of all of it.

'It's like nine hundred feet high,' I said, remembering what I'd heard from my French teacher sophomore year. 'I think there's a restaurant up there.'

'I have always wanted to go.' She sounded lost and alone.

'First the 40/40 Club, now the Eiffel Tower.' The joke came off weak, even to me. 'You're not exactly a cheap date, you know that?'

'I want to die there.'

I looked at her, startled. 'What?'

'You heard me.'

'Not today.'

She didn't say anything. I didn't either, for a while. Gobi tucked her chin and closed her eyes. As she leaned back against my shoulder, her coat slipped open and I caught a glimpse of the Glock, hanging out for the whole world to see.

'Jeez, Gobi –' I reached over to push the gun back out of view and pull her coat shut, but when my hand brushed the harness, she snapped violently awake, shoved me back, and grabbed the gun, then held it out, pointing it right at me.

'Gobi.' I tried to make my voice calm. 'What are you doing? Put that down.'

She didn't move. Her face was absolutely blank, an alabaster mask with real eyes twitching around inside it. A thin trickle of blood had started running from her left nostril. I couldn't tell how many of the other passengers had noticed what was going on, but the woman across from us in a business suit – a middle-aged Parisian executive who looked like she was on her way out to a power lunch – was staring straight at Gobi and the Glock.

'Hey,' I said, 'it's okay. It's Perry.' I held up my hands. 'You're just confused. Just put the gun down, okay?'

All around us, people were starting to panic, jumping out of their seats, one or two of them screaming, getting out cell phones, fighting to get out of the railway car. I tried not to let any of that faze me, struggling to keep my expression calm. The hole at the end of the gun's barrel looked as big as the Holland Tunnel.

In front of me, Gobi was talking to herself, saying something low in Lithuanian, murmuring it under her breath, a flurry of consonants and vowels, her pupils flicking around so fast that her eyes themselves seemed to be trembling in their sockets. The exhaustion and unreality of the moment made it feel like I had a clear bubble enveloping my head, as if everything were happening at one level of detachment. I fought to think clearly, but at the moment clarity was in extremely short supply.

You must promise me . . .

'Zusane,' I said. 'Zusane Elzbieta Zaksauskas.'

She narrowed her eyes at the sound of that other name, the blind hysteria starting to waver, giving way to suspicious uncertainty, but the gun stayed where it was. At the far end of the car, people were staring at us, holding their breath.

'You are last target,' she said.

'No,' I said. 'You know I'm not.'

She flicked off the safety. 'I must finish.'

'It's Perry. It's me.'

She murmured another phrase in her own language, finger tightening on the trigger. Now her eyes were almost closed, as if she didn't want to see what was going to happen next, but her lips kept moving. It almost sounded like she was praying.

The voice in my head spoke with absolute certainty: *She's going to shoot me. I'm going to die right here on the Metro in a country where I don't even speak the language.* And at that same moment, I remembered the words that Erich had told me back in Zermatt.

'*Zusane,*' I said. '*As tave myliu.*'

Her eyes widened for a moment, and then finally the gun started to go down. We were slowing, moving into the station, and every other passenger on the car was shoved up against the door, waiting for it to open.

I kept my full attention on Gobi. After what felt like forever, she seemed to collapse back into herself again, a storm of emotions spilling over her face, and when she blinked at me, she looked like she was crying.

'Perry?'

'It's okay.'

'Why did you say that?' She looked at the gun in her hand, then back up at me with a dawning realization and a sense of horror.

'I don't know,' I said. 'I don't even know what it means.'

'It is . . . nothing.' She looked at me and now her eyes were clear.

The train had stopped. I let my gaze stray out the window at the flood of frightened passengers putting as much distance between us and them as humanly possible. I didn't hear any police sirens, not yet, but they were inevitable.

'Come on,' I said. 'We have to get out of here, now.'

I put my arm around her shoulder, took the Glock and shoved it under my own coat, then wiped the blood from under her nose. She was still bleeding as I hustled her out onto the platform and up the stairs to the street in the rain.

41

'Teenagers' – My Chemical Romance

We didn't talk all the way up the rue Oberkampf. The rain kept pouring down harder than ever, splattering in puddles and making miniature waterfalls down canopies of cafés, keeping most of the pedestrians off the street. Scooters and big blue city buses roared past, splashing dirty water up from the gutter. I bought an umbrella from a street vendor and held it low over our faces, checking the reflections in shop windows to figure out if we were being followed.

Halfway down the next block, we passed a Chinese place, approaching the dark wooden exterior of the Café Charbon and a narrow purple awning next to it reading:

NOUVEAU CASINO

CONCERTS

CLUBBING

I opened the door and a tall, skinny-to-the-point-of-skeletal man standing there in a striped hoodie looked up from his iPod. *'Ou allez-vous?'*

'I need to go in.'

'No. Not open till tonight.'

'I'm with the band.' I pointed at the flier stapled in the doorway. 'Inchworm?'

'You are . . .' He kept looking at me, swiveling his head from one side to the other, as if there were some angle at which my arrival here would fit his expectations. 'With that band?'

'That's right.' I mimed a few chords. 'Bass player.'

The bouncer glanced at Gobi leaning against me with my coat over her shoulders. She must have looked punk rock enough for him, because he made a flicking gesture down the hallway and we stepped inside, down into the club.

That was when a hand swung out and took hold of my shoulder, stopping me in my tracks.

'Didn't I tell you?' Linus practically shouted. Beneath the huge cloud of his white hair, veins were standing out in his head. 'Didn't I tell you that miserable wench was going to ruin everything?'

We were still in the entryway, not five feet off the sidewalk, Gobi and I on one side while Linus stood in front of us in the middle of a full-tilt rant.

'Linus,' I said, 'you were talking about tour percentages. Paula was literally trying to kill me.'

'Six percent of the door – I'd say she was trying to kill all of us!'

'I mean, with an actual gun.'

'Whatever.' He waved his hand. 'Just like I told the boys, Inchworm is finishing this tour. I always knew Armitage was a thug. So what? It's a ruthless business. You think David Geffen is a saint? That changes nothing.' He shook his head. 'These local promoters are paying us, and we're going to play. With the Slippery When Wet Tour back in 'eighty-six, when Jon Bon Jovi got a chest cold, did we go home with our tails between our legs? Hell no, and we're not going home now.'

I looked over his shoulder. 'Right now I think we'd just like to go inside.'

Linus, still muttering, led us into the club. Even mostly deserted, without the lights and strobes going, Nouveau Casino was a visually disorienting experience, a wide-open room with harlequin-colored walls and ceilings made out of irregular geometric shapes. Off to one side was a DJ booth and a red suede bar with an old-fashioned glass chandelier that looked like it could have been pilfered by the Nazis from the palace of Versailles and abandoned here during the liberation by mistake.

The band was onstage in the middle of yet another soundcheck. When Norrie saw us coming, he stopped pounding the drums, dropped his sticks, and practically fell over his cymbals on the way to the footlights.

'Huh-Holy shit – *Perry?*' Then, recognizing Gobi, he raised both his hands in a frantic warding-off gesture, took a step back, and almost tripped over Caleb's amp. 'Whuh-Whoa, no.' His eyes were wide open, and his stutter, which always had the cruel tendency to act up in moments of stress, went absolutely berserk. It almost sounded like he was rapping. 'Guh-Guh-Get her out of here, muh-man. I'm nuh-nuh-not even fuh-fuh-fucking around with you – juh-juh-hust get her out of here *now*.'

'It's okay,' I said. 'She's all right.'

'Shuh-She's a fuh-fuh-hucking buh-bullet muh-magnet! A-And I duh-don't wuh-want her here!'

'Hey, it's Perry the Platypus!' Sasha dropped the microphone and came down to the floor, threw his arms around me in a big stinky road hug. He smelled like a mixture of hair product, Cool Ranch Doritos, and Coke Zero, and even though I'd just seen him two days earlier, I felt such a sudden huge wave of homesickness well up over me all at once that I wanted to cry. 'What's up, Baron von Broheim? That was *waaaay* crazy back in Venice, huh? What are you doing here?'

'Just in the neighborhood,' I said, and mentally added, *Jeopardizing my family's lives . . . again.*

Sasha cackled and punched me in the arm. '"In the neighborhood," he said . . . Will you listen to this fart-knocker?' A giant grin had spread over his face, making him look about twelve years old. 'Hey, you better go talk to Linus. I think he really wants to, you know, work some shit out.'

'We talked.'

'Cool. I love Europe, man. I'm moving here.' He turned to Gobi, ecstatic enough now that his words were running together without the added inconvenience of punctuation. 'And you're here too, the original European *chick,* that's *so* utterly cool since you're kind of the reason all of it happened in the first place and you guys are too cute together, like Sid and Nancy except without the drugs – hey, Caleb, Norrie, did you see who's here?'

'I suh-saw,' Norrie muttered, and Caleb, who had just now gotten his Strat tuned the way he wanted it, gave us a distracted wave, as if all of this were happening in his garage on a slow Tuesday after school.

'So' – Sasha clapped his hands again – 'are you ready to rawk?'

'Not exactly.'

Norrie took a step forward. 'Wuh-What's guh-going on, Perry?'

'I need to talk to you guys in private,' I said, and when I took off my coat, the Glock fell out of my pocket and we stood there staring at it like it was a dead bird on the floor.

'No,' Norrie said. 'Nuh-No. No way. *No.*'

'Norrie.'

'No. No!'

'Dude.' I'd already picked up the gun and stuffed it back in my parka, but I kept seeing Norrie's eyes flick back to the lump that it made in my pocket. 'I need your help.'

We were leaning against the side of the stage while Sasha and Caleb tried to figure out the set list. Gobi was sitting on the floor beside me with her head in her hands. She hadn't moved or spoken since we'd gone off to this dark corner of the club.

'Just let us – '

'I duh-don't even care about the shuh-show,' Norrie said. 'I juh-hust don't want to guh-get *killed.*'

'Trust me, man, okay?'

He looked at me wearily. We'd been friends since grade school, and we'd been through a lot together, and this wasn't how I wanted to catch up with him again. We should've been at home in his basement listening to Wolfmother, playing Red Dead Redemption, and talking about Princeton and girls and whatever else popped into our heads. Even back in high school, I'd known it couldn't last forever, but I hadn't ever dreamed that it would end so crashingly soon.

'And wuh-why c-can't you just guh-go to the cops about this again?' Norrie asked, then answered his own question. 'Oh yeah, thuh-that's right, buh-because yuh-you're traveling with a *h-hired assassin!*'

'Look,' I said. 'I'll have the cops here tonight. I just want as much cover as possible if something goes wrong.'

'You w-want to have an armed st-standoff in the middle of our show,' he said, sounding abruptly very sick of being my best friend. 'Again.'

'What about that song?'

He stared at me, his face screwed up with confusion. 'Whuh-What?'

'You said that you wrote a new song.'

'Are you suh-serious?'

'Let's hear it.'

'Nuh-*now?*'

I looked around the empty club, thinking of everything that was happening out beyond those walls, thinking of me and Gobi and my family, the odds against us stacked higher than they'd ever been. 'Might be our last chance.'

'No. No way.' Shaking his head. 'I cuh-can't –'

'Yeah, you can.'

Norrie took in a breath, shook his head, and with a long-suffering, oh-Lord-I-can't-believe-I'm-doing-this sigh of exasperation, turned and went back to the stage, where Caleb and Sasha had been studiously pretending they weren't eavesdropping on our conversation. He murmured something to them as he got behind his drum kit, picked up his sticks, and fired off a three-click beat as Caleb ripped into the first notes.

The song – what he had of it – was ragged, unpolished, sloppy, all over the place . . . and unquestionably the best thing that Norrie had ever written. Midway through the second makeshift verse, unable to hold back any longer, I climbed up and grabbed the replacement bass that was sitting there, plugged it in, and started improvising a bass line on the spot, making my way up to the microphone to do backup vocals with Sasha.

When we finished, Gobi and Linus were standing there staring at the foot of the stage with matching expressions of amazement. I wiped the sweat out of my eyes and looked past Caleb, toward where Norrie had just finished pounding out the last beat of the song. He was gazing up me.

'Well?' he managed. 'What do you think?'

'Yeah.'

'Yeah?'

'Yeah.'

'I call it "Bullet Magnet."'

I nodded. 'Good title.'

'I thought so.'

'Me too.'

The applause from the back of the room startled us all.

42

'Baby Goes to Eleven' – Superdrag

'Stormaire?' Paula's voice rang out loud and clear through the excellent acoustics of the empty concert hall. She pulled out a lighter and held it up. 'Rock on, baby.'

I put down the bass and saw her at the back of the club. She was wearing a black wool coat and knee-high leather boots, standing by the bar, with Monash to her right in a gray business suit. Between them, the cadaverous Parisian bouncer that had let us in a few minutes earlier stood with his skinny tattooed arms crossed, cupping his elbows and trying really hard to look defiant and French, which could not have been easy given the pistol that Monash was pointing at his head.

'Listen,' Paula said. 'I know you were planning something special for tonight, but Dad and I are kind of pressed for time here. Mind stepping out back with us for a moment? I *really* think you'll want to see this.' She started to turn around, then glanced back almost as an afterthought: 'Oh, and bring the freak.'

Gobi looked at me, and we followed Paula out of the club.

A white FedEx truck was parked in an alleyway next to a row of scooters. Rain had soaked the piles of trash back here, and the whole place smelled like raw sewage. Without a word, Paula walked around to the back of the truck and opened the doors, standing out of the way so that I could see inside.

And then, in real time, I saw them.

Three hunched figures sitting there on the floor against the inside wall of the truck, squinting up into the light. And all of a sudden I felt everything else lurch up inside of me and melt away to nothing.

'Mom,' I said. 'Dad. Annie.'

My mother was the first one to react. She moved forward

and threw her arms around me. 'Perry, thank God.' Just hearing that tone in her voice, I realized that she was even more worried about me than she was for herself or Annie. Dad was on his knees, holding on to Annie, kind of helping her move forward out of the van.

'Are you guys okay?'

Dad nodded. 'We're fine.' His voice was quiet, different, broken somehow, without a trace of the confidence that I naturally associated with him. His stubble had grown into the beginnings of a beard, making him look completely different, younger and much older at the same time. 'We're tired.'

'Annie?' I gave her a big hug. 'You all right, munchkin?'

She nodded and hugged me back so tightly that I could feel her heart racing. 'I hate you, big brother.'

'Yeah,' I said, 'I deserve it.'

'You owe me *so* big for this.'

'You're right,' I said. 'When this is over . . .'

'Just as long as it *is* over.' There were tears in her eyes. 'That would be enough.'

'I want to thank you for holding up your end of the deal, Stormaire,' Paula cut in behind me, and when I turned,

I saw that she had replaced the Glock that she'd lost to Gobi with something even uglier, some kind of customized Soviet-looking machine pistol pointed at Gobi's face.

Monash had Gobi backed up against the alley wall under a quaint piece of Parisian graffiti depicting schoolchildren playing 'Ring Around the Rosie' around a mushroom cloud. Rain from the rooftops was trickling down, making Gobi's pale face shine in all kinds of radiant, unhealthy ways. 'You brought her in to us, just like you said you would.'

Gobi's eyes flashed over Paula's shoulder and latched hard on to mine, magnet to steel, and I shook my head violently.

'No,' I said. 'Wait a second, that's not –'

'You made the right choice,' Paula said. 'After all, who wouldn't choose their own family over some girl he hardly knows?'

'That wasn't how I planned it,' I said, but Gobi wasn't looking at me anymore.

'We're not going to lose her this time,' Monash said. It was the first time I'd heard him speak, not counting all the shouting inside the steamer trunk back in Venice. Now that he had a gun in his hand, his voice was refined, British American, the product of private school and board rooms, exactly the way you'd expect the father of someone like Paula to sound.

Tucking the weapon into a shoulder holster, letting Paula keep her gun pointed at Gobi, he started strapping a pair of plastic restraints around Gobi's wrists. 'And there's going to be quite a lengthy re-education process, isn't that right, Zusane?' And then, to Paula: 'We've got an empire to rebuild, darling.'

Gobi lowered her head and said something under her breath.

'What's that, love?'

'My name is Gobija.'

The restraints zipped tighter. At first I thought she was going to do the same thing she'd done in Zermatt, going quietly until she had a chance to assess the situation.

I was wrong.

43

'Icky Thump' – The White Stripes

The noise Gobi's head made as it smashed into Monash's nose was kind of a wet, muffled crack, like what you'd get if you pulverized a grapefruit inside a burlap bag. Monash didn't get a chance to cry out. By then, she was already on him, looping her arms up and wrapping the restraints around his neck, crossing her wrists and jerking them tight. Something popped in Monash's spine – something deep and fragile and important-sounding – and he let out a sharp glottal croak and started twitching frantically in his five-thousand-dollar suit.

Gobi whirled, still in motion, keeping Monash's body upright in front of her, ramming him forward like a human shield into Paula, who had backed up, trying to get a shot. Even I saw that wasn't going to happen. The alley was narrow, with even less space now that the FedEx truck was parked here, and no room to maneuver if Paula wasn't planning on shooting Gobi through her father, who was arguably still alive and kicking. My parents and Annie had already jumped back up inside the truck.

'Hold it!' a voice shouted down the alley, and when I glanced back, I saw Nolan running toward us up the alley from rue Oberkampf with two uniformed gendarmes coming up behind him.

• . • ‑ ◆

I've watched the surveillance footage of what happened in the next nineteen seconds, from several different angles – the CIA made me go over it with them, and a bootleg version is also available on YouTube, and I still haven't wrapped my mind around it.

Things start to get blurry around the one-minute mark. Then around 1:22, you can see Gobi pivot with Monash still held up in front of her like a spastic puppet. At 1:29, there's a gunshot – it's Paula's, and it's headed nowhere in particular, ricocheting off the alley wall where the cops will later find it embedded in a trash can thirty meters away – and the driver's-side door of the FedEx truck flings open, knocking Paula over sideways. I'm out of the frame at this point, temporarily blocked out by Nolan and the gendarmes, who are still charging forward until they realize somebody's shooting.

At 1:33, Paula regains her balance, turns around, and fires a second shot, this one more deliberate, but too late. There's a flicker of something moving into the truck, the door slamming shut.

If you pause the footage at 1:38, you can see my face pop back up in the foreground, looking straight up. The expression on my face says it all.

The truck is gone.

So is my family.

So is Gobi.

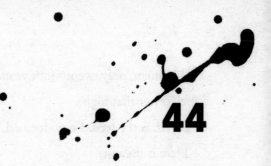

44

'Walking Far from Home' – Iron & Wine

Which brings us here, Gobi.

Not quite, but close enough.

With everything that's been written and broadcast and blogged about us in those final few hours in Paris, official and otherwise, you would think that the full story had been mapped out. And to the extent that the facts tell the story, that's true. There were definitely aspects of the investigation that Nolan's people withheld from the public, especially when the lead was still flying and the blood was still wet, but none of that really affected the outcome in any concrete way.

In the end it boiled down to this:

A woman, only twenty-four years old, died on top of the Eiffel Tower that night.

As far as the record is concerned, those are the facts.

Here is the rest.

● ● ● ●

The wet metal railing is flaking nine hundred feet up, rusty, worn smooth in places from the millions of eager hands that have gripped it over the years, gazing down over the lights of Paris. It's so cold up here that I already can't feel my fingertips, even with my hands stuffed down in the pockets of my parka. I stopped feeling my earlobes and the tip of my nose somewhere on the elevator ride to the top.

Despite the darkness and the temperature, plenty of tourists are still milling around up here posing for pictures, pointing out landmarks far below in a half-dozen different languages. Being here makes them feel glamorous somehow, part of something bigger than themselves. They act like celebrities at a photo shoot. They pose and preen. They air-kiss and vamp. They've got bottled water and hot chocolate and sandwiches from the bistro and plastic bags from the souvenir shop one floor below the main observation deck. There have been no additional security checks at ticket windows tonight, and why would there be? The afternoon's assault off the rue Oberkampf was an isolated incident, the identity of its sole fatality not yet released to the public, but certainly not a cause for panic in the City of Lights. No one has mentioned anything to the authorities about keeping an eye on the Eiffel Tower in particular, because if such a person were to do that, neither one of us could have come up here.

I never would have seen you again.

And I see you now.

• . •- •

You're standing twenty yards away, waiting for me on the opposite side of the platform with your arms crossed and your back to the railing. We're a thousand feet above the most beautiful city in the world, and you're only looking at me.

The wind and rain blow hard in my face, making my eyes water a little, and when I come closer and wipe them clear, I can see you're bleeding. Not much, not yet. It's running down your face from your right nostril. From here, I can't tell whether you recognize me or not.

'Gobi.'

You smile sadly. You say something in Lithuanian. It sounds like a prayer.

'Where did you leave the FedEx van?'

You blink and gaze back at me.

'Where's my family?'

Your eyes flick down and up to me again, almost tentatively, but without true recognition. It's as if you've spotted someone in an airport, an old acquaintance whose face is familiar but whose name you can't recall.

'I know you like them,' I say. 'I know you'd never do anything to hurt them. Just tell me where they are.'

You smile again, then wince and touch your head, as if it suddenly hurts very badly.

'My mom and dad and my little sister, Annie,' I say. 'You know them. You can picture their faces.'

You just shake your head.

Then, a few seconds later, you pull out the gun.

'Stand Up' – The Prodigy

I don't know when the police showed up. All it took was one particularly observant Tokyo schoolgirl somewhere off to our left to spot the pistol in Gobi's hand and make a phone call, and within five minutes the observation platform had been cleared.

Then it was just us and the cops. For a long moment Gobi and I stood there watching Avenue Anatole France fill with police lights, turning it into a river of flickering blue along the truer, darker curve of the Seine itself. The next time the elevator door opened, it dispatched a wedge of gendarmes in what looked like full riot gear.

But when they saw what Gobi was doing with the gun,

they kept on their side of the platform. One of them shouted something, and it doesn't matter that I slept through two years of high school French – I got the gist. Let him go. Put it down. Hands up. All of that. Gobi ignored them completely, focusing all her attention on me.

'*As tave myliu*,' Gobi said. With her free hand, she reached out and brushed the wet hair out of my eyes. 'Your hair is getting shaggy, *mielasis*.' Then she pointed the pistol back at my head, underneath my chin.

'It doesn't have to go this way.'

'Yes, it does.'

'Just tell me what you've done with my family. Tell me where they are.'

'One more must die.'

'Gobi, no, you're sick. There's a tumor in your brain. You're not thinking clearly. Like on the train.'

'*Au revoir.*'

'Gobi.' I held up my hands. 'You don't need to do this anymore. *As tave myliu.*'

Something changed in her eyes, not much, maybe just a subtle shift in the lights reflected in her pupils. I kissed her then, not even thinking about the gun, while she kept it jammed up to my chin. Her mouth felt as cold as the metal barrel against my skin, her lips coming open and kissing me, the surprising warmth of her tongue, salty-sweet as it slipped inside and slid against mine. The gun was still there, pushing up hard against my jaw.

'How did you learn to say "I love you" in Lithuanian?' she asked.

'Erich.'

'You are still jealous of him.'

I shook my head. 'No.'

She put her lips to my ear. 'Sixty-six rue de Turenne,' she murmured. 'Is parking garage. They're in the back.'

'Thank you.'

'And Perry.'

'Yes?'

'I am sorry.'

'Wh–'

She moved the gun from my head and put it against her own, placing the barrel to her temple. Too late, I saw how it was going to end.

'Gobi, no!'

She pulled the trigger.

Nothing happened.

I stared at her. She looked back at me.

'The safety.' I said. 'It's still on. You forgot – '

Then from somewhere behind me, a dark shape flew forward and crashed into her, knocking her to the floor of the platform.

• . ✦ ⁃ ●

Sitting up, I saw Gobi on her back, turning sideways, grappling with the dark-garbed figure on top of her. I saw the shining glint of buckles and a badge. One of the gendarmes had broken ranks, jumped out into the rain, and tackled her.

Gobi squirmed sideways, reared back, and released a kick to the face that spun the gendarme a hundred and eighty degrees around, hard enough to knock the riot helmet from the officer's head, revealing a spray of blond hair.

Paula.

In less than a second, Paula had already caught her balance, recovering from the kick, and reached into the uniform she was wearing to pull out an automatic. She held it in the textbook two-handed grip, pointing it at Gobi.

'Paula,' I said.

She glanced back at the gendarmes. 'Tonight I bought your lives – rented them for a few moments, anyway.'

'What do you mean?'

'When the reports came across the police band, I got out here as soon as I could.' Her eyes flicked back to the group of gendarmes on the far side of the platform, and Paula reached into her tunic and pulled out a laminated ID badge on a lanyard. 'Interpol special hostage negotiation squad.'

'Very realistic,' I said.

'It comes in handy from time to time. The police have orders to stand down until I say otherwise.'

I tried to smile. It didn't hurt too much. 'I didn't know you still cared.'

'You're sweet.' Paula drew in a breath of night air. 'But deluded as always.' She took a step toward Gobi. 'Zusane. You know, the last thing my father said before he died today was "Make her suffer." I promised him that I would.' Paula regarded her with pity bordering on revulsion. 'But . . . look at you. Christ. You're half dead already. You can't even stand up. You're rotten with cancer. At this point, anything I do to you would be a mercy.'

Gobi didn't say anything. Still keeping the pistol trained on her, Paula looked out to the southeast, at the long stretch of open, flat field leading off to the Tour Montparnasse. 'You know what that is? The Champ de Mars.' She glanced back at Gobi. 'Named after the god of war.'

'Then they should bury us both there,' Gobi said.

Paula shook her head again. 'Just you.'

I held up my hand. 'Paula – '

Paula squeezed the trigger.

The first shot slammed into Gobi's chest, the second her belly, driving her backwards against the guardrail with the force of the gunshot. She didn't make a sound, her expression not betraying a hint of what it must have felt like at that moment. It was as though she was just putting the pain somewhere completely away from her, a private place where all the hurt went. I saw her fingers grope for the railing as she tried to hoist herself up to keep fighting, and that was when Paula fired again, hitting Gobi in the left knee. Gobi's leg went out from under her and this time she stayed down, palms upraised, fingers outstretched.

Her hands were empty.

Paula kicked the Glock aside and stood over her with her own pistol aimed point-blank at Gobi's face. My hearing was gone in my left ear from the gunshots. Paula's mouth was moving, shouting loudly enough that I could almost make it out, something about her father, something about the end of it all.

'Leave her alone,' I said, but I couldn't hear myself, and then I realized that Paula probably couldn't hear me either.

I stood up.

• . ● ●

According to Erich Schoeneweiss, in order to successfully break a board or brick in tae kwon do, the hand has to be traveling about thirty feet per second when it makes contact. Mustering this kind of speed requires the puncher to be aiming beyond the object, punching through it in the direction of something on the other side.

I aimed for the back of Paula's head.

I punched a hole in the night.

When Paula went down, it was all at once. The gun slipped from her hands and her face swung forward, deflected off the guardrail, snapped back, and came around showing me a dentist's nightmare of blood and broken teeth. Yet somehow it was still a grin.

'Like father, like son,' she said. It came out a little mushy, but I could make out the words just the same through my one good ear. 'Your dad liked to tussle too, Perry – did you know that?'

I tried to tell her to shut up and realized I needed to catch my breath. I'd put everything I had into the punch and it hadn't been enough. While she was talking, Paula was already scrambling around looking for the gun, either hers or Gobi's, but it was dark and the platform was black and one of her eyes was already swelling shut.

'I always thought it was funny. You were so nervous about taking me to bed' – she wiped the blood from her mouth with her sleeve – 'when the whole time I was getting everything I needed from your old man. Ask him about it, Perry. Ask him how I was. Too bad you'll never find out for yourself.'

I went over to where Gobi was lying and put my arms around her. I could smell a sheared copper smell coming from her wounds, a deep, wet, desperate smell like scorched fabric and cauterized skin.

'It's okay,' I said. 'You don't have to do any more.'

'Perry.' She put her mouth right next to my good ear. 'Lift me up.'

'Are you sure?'

She nodded. She was heavy, much heavier than I remembered from before, and the phrase *dead weight* sprang to mind, although maybe I was just weaker than I remembered – that was almost certainly the case. Somehow I got my hands underneath her arms and lifted her upright. I could feel the rough, ragged scrape of her breathing, her broken ribs rubbing together in her chest as I held her there.

A few feet in front of us, Paula rose up. Through the blood and the swelling, the fire in her eyes was a reflection of something fierce, some gaudy spectacle of vengeance that only she could see. She had both guns, Gobi's in her right hand, hers in her left.

'Sorry,' Paula said. 'This is it for us.'

I felt Gobi's shoulders stiffen with anticipation. I braced

my legs to support her. Leaning all her weight back against me, she swung her right leg straight up in the air, then brought it down on Paula's neck.

The ax kick connected exactly where it had to, dead center across the base of the skull, and when Paula's face hit the floor, it was with more weight than she'd ever carried when she was alive.

I looked down at her lying there in the rain, eyes open, blank, staring.

I caught Gobi and lay her down slowly beside me, running my hands through her hair. It was dark and it was raining, and that was how we stayed, the two of us huddled together next to the metal railing until the gendarmes came out and led us away.

'Brand New Friend' – Lloyd Cole and the Commotions

'Hey, kid.'

I was sitting in the otherwise empty waiting room in the American Hospital in Paris with the television on. I didn't have to take my eyes off the French version of *Biggest Loser* to see who had just walked in. Agent Nolan stood there in the doorway for a long beat, holding his briefcase, waiting to be acknowledged.

'You gonna say hi to me?'

'Sorry.' I turned my other ear toward him, the one that I could still hear out of. 'Speak into this one.'

'Where's the family?'

'In a hotel,' I said. It was basically true. I decided Nolan didn't need to be informed that my parents were staying in separate hotels on opposite sides of the Seine. There were some things that even the CIA didn't need to know.

'What about the band?'

'They went back to New York yesterday with our manager.'

'And you? Flying home soon?'

'Tomorrow,' I said, 'probably,' and started to reach for the remote.

Nolan looked back up the hall toward the OR. 'How long's she been in surgery?'

'Thirteen hours. They're finishing now.'

'They get all of it?'

'What do you care?'

'Crazy, huh?'

'What's that?'

'She's wearing a bulletproof vest up there, saving her life, and the whole time it was the tumor that was killing her.'

He started to say something, and I turned my bad ear back toward him. When he saw me do that, he walked straight in front of me, blocking the TV set.

'Listen, Perry. Maybe we got off on the wrong foot. Maybe you got a rough lesson in gunboat diplomacy – who knows?' He shrugged. 'That part I asked you before about her . . . I was just being polite. I already talked to the neurosurgeons. They said she's in a coma.'

'Induced,' I said.

'What?'

'It's an induced coma. It's what they do to protect higher brain function during and immediately after major neurosurgery.'

'Somebody's been reading his Wikipedia.'

I switched off the TV and looked at him. 'Why are you here?'

'As a matter of fact . . .' He sighed and sat down next to me, plucking at the seams of his suit pants. 'I want to help.'

'Unless you can give me back the hearing in my left ear or . . .' – I almost said 'save my parents' marriage' – 'undo what happened here, you're pretty useless to me.'

'I never said I wanted to help you personally,' Nolan said. 'Although in this particular situation, I might be in the position to do so.' He opened his briefcase and took out a thick stack of official-looking documents, some of them in

English, others in French. 'Nobody knows how your little Lithuanian princess is going to come out of surgery, or if she's going to come out at all. Even the docs say it's too soon to tell. But one thing's for sure: At the end of the day, somebody's gonna get stuck with a hell of a hospital bill. We're talking millions in rehab, all that shit. She'll be in debt for the rest of her life.'

'Let me guess,' I said. 'You can take care of that.'

'The agency could. Probably.' He was looking at me out of the corner of his eye. 'In exchange for certain considerations.'

'Forget it,' I said.

'Easy, kid. Let's not get ahead of ourselves. At this point we don't even know if she's going to make it. And if she does?' Another shrug. 'She might not be able to shoot straight. But we're willing to take that risk.'

'That's big of you.'

'Hey, like I said, we do what we can. In any case, in the spirit of starting over, I want to just let you know, Uncle Sam's got this one. Whatever it takes to get her back on her feet.' He grinned. 'Alive and kicking, am I right?'

'Agent Nolan.'

'Yeah, kid?'

'And I mean this from the bottom of my heart – '

'Yeah?'

'Go fuck yourself.'

He snapped his briefcase shut and stood up.

'That's not friendly, Perry.' His voice was cordial but just barely, as if every word was costing him a little bit of dignity. 'I extended the hand of friendship and you just pissed on it.'

'Maybe I was just practicing some gunboat diplomacy.'

'Hey, no harm, no foul.' Now his grin was tighter, narrower, seeming to flatten out the broad planes of his face. 'No matter who pays, we're on her. You know that, right? If Zusane Zaksauskas does walk out of here, there's not a place on this planet that she can hide from us. She's ours for life.'

'Lucky her.'

He snorted and started for the door. What stopped him was the surgeon in scrubs and a mask and hairnet standing in the entryway. He glanced at Nolan, and then at me.

'Perry?' the doctor said.

I stood up, felt my heart vault upward into my throat. 'Yes?'

'I'm afraid I've got some bad news.'

I stared at him, and Nolan stared at him, and I could feel the air molecules in the room fall absolutely motionless around us.

'We did everything we could,' the surgeon said, 'but she never recovered consciousness after the operation. I am very sorry.'

Nolan sighed and shook his head, then looked back at me. 'Sorry about that, kid. Like I said before, though, it's probably for the best.'

After he left, the surgeon took off his mask and looked at me.

'I thought you told me you weren't a doctor,' I said.

'What is your American saying?' Erich tapped his finger against his head. '"I play one on TV"?'

'So Gobi . . .'

'The body seems to have mysteriously disappeared. Or soon will.'

'I take it you'll be making the proper arrangements?'

'*Ja*,' Erich said. 'Is already taken care of.'

47

'We Own the Sky' – M83

The day after Gobija Zaksauskas was officially declared dead for the second time in her life, her remains whisked away from the hospital morgue by persons unknown, my mom and Annie and I flew back to the States. My dad stayed in Paris to catch a later flight. How much later remained to be seen. He didn't tell us, and nobody asked.

Walking through customs at JFK, Mom stopped and looked at the Christmas tree in the international terminal.

'We missed Thanksgiving,' she said, in a funny voice, like she was just now realizing how far away we'd been. I knew how she felt. America sounded loud and frantic in my one good ear, people running, shouting, flights being announced in a barrage of noise and information. All around us, time had passed, and we'd been plunged right back into the flow again, trying to get our balance.

Then, like that, it was December.

Annie and I spent a lot of time at home over the next few weeks, going to movies, playing board games, wrapping Christmas presents, and downloading holiday music. Even the most normal, boring American things felt reassuring somehow, like they were anchoring us into place.

Nobody said much about my dad. I tried to say something once or twice to Annie about it, but she didn't seem to want to talk, so I let it go. My mom said she didn't care about getting a tree this year, so Annie and I went out and brought one home ourselves on top of the Volvo while she was at work. Norrie, Caleb, and Sasha came over and helped us decorate it, stringing popcorn and cranberries because Annie had always wanted to do that. We practiced some of the new material and even did a couple of Christmas songs with Annie singing the background vocals on 'Santa Claus Is

Back in Town.' Mom said it sounded nice, but it was in that distracted kind of voice that could have been referring to anything, or nothing at all. She was being too quiet, spending too much time alone, but there didn't seem to be any way to mention it.

Two weeks after our arrival back in New York, Chow came home from Berkeley on Christmas break. He stopped by the house one night for pizza and eggnog. Naturally, he'd read about everything that happened with me and Gobi in Europe and couldn't wait to talk about it – ever since we'd come home, it was all over the news and the Internet and everywhere else.

It was good to see him again, and we stayed up late into the night, talking by the fire. He told me that while they were home, he and his old high school flame were back together 'on a temporary basis,' which as far as I could tell meant they'd started sleeping together until they had to go back to their respective colleges in January.

'What about you, dawg?' he said, looking over at the Christmas tree. 'Another Christmas at home with your red lights and your blue balls?'

After everything that had happened, it was a pretty

freaking insensitive thing to say, but I found myself laughing, and that felt good.

For a long time, I was afraid I'd forgotten how.

• • •

Then, two days before Christmas, my dad came home.

He called from the airport, and showed up at the house that night with a full beard and a bag of gifts like Santa except without the laughs. It was all very civil, very polite, and completely jarring. Mom stayed on her side of the couch, he stayed on his. At the end of the world's most awkward conversation, he said goodbye, hugged me and Annie, and started back for his hotel.

I wanted to say, 'Dad, wait.'

I wanted to ask him what really happened with Paula. I wanted to hear his side of the story. There had to be a reason for what he'd done, right?

Someday I want to hear it.

• • •

'You coming downstairs?' Mom asked. 'Your sister's making hot cocoa and she wants to watch *Elf*.'

I glanced up from the computer. 'Maybe in a while.' It was Christmas Eve, and I was not much in the holiday spirit despite a prediction of scattered flurries tonight and Death Cab for Cutie on the radio doing their version of 'Baby Please Come Home.'

I looked down at the online application for next fall's admission to UCLA. It was only half finished, and I didn't have the strength to seek out one more letter of recommendation. I knew I had to finish it, though. It was time to move forward, to aim past it and punch through. I thought maybe California was far enough away to get a new start.

'Oh, I almost forgot,' Mom said. 'This came for you.'

I looked at the envelope she'd dropped on my desk. There was no return address. I looked at the blurry postmark. It looked like Fiji.

I tore it open.

It was a Christmas card from the Hotel Schoeneweiss, showing a huge crowd of men and women in Santa suits trying to climb a wooden pole in the annual ClauWau competition in Zermatt. Inside was blank, except for two lines of block print at the bottom.

NEW LOCATION FOR THE HOTEL. ONLY ONE
GUEST SO FAR. SHE HAS ASKED TO SEE YOU
NEXT TIME YOU ARE IN THE ISLANDS.

It was initialed with the letters ES.

I tucked it in my desk along with my passport, slid the drawer shut, and went downstairs to the smell of hot cocoa, to join Annie and my mom.